INFECTED

INFECTED

SOPHIE LITTLEFIELD

DELACORTE PRESS

Text copyright © 2015 by Sophie Littlefield
Jacket art copyright © 2015 by Tom Sanderson

All rights reserved. Published in the United States by Delacorte Press, an imprint of Random House Children's Books, a division of Random House LLC, a Penguin Random House Company, New York.

Delacorte Press is a registered trademark and the colophon is a trademark of Random House LLC.

Visit us on the Web! randomhouse.com/teens

Educators and librarians, for a variety of teaching tools, visit us at RHTeachersLibrarians.com

Library of Congress Cataloging-in-Publication Data
Littlefield, Sophie.
    Infected / Sophie Littlefield.—First edition.
        pages cm
    Summary; Carina, a high school track star and the niece of a scientist whose research deadly agents will do anything to obtain, is injected with a performance-enhancing drug that will kill her unless she can find the antidote in twenty-four hours.
    ISBN 978-0-385-74106-4 (hc : alk. paper) — ISBN 978-0-375-98357-3 (ebook)
    [1. Survival—Fiction. 2. Spies—Fiction. 3. Dating (Social customs)—Fiction.] I. Title.
    PZ7.L7359In 2015
    [Fic]—dc23
                        2013046923

The text of this book is set in 11.5-point Caslon Book BE.
Book design by Stephanie Moss

Printed in the United States of America
10 9 8 7 6 5 4 3 2 1
First Edition

Random House Children's Books supports the First Amendment and celebrates the right to read.

For Elliot Granick Wiecek

INFECTED

CHAPTER ONE

Friday, 3:45 p.m.
14:08:55

"Black Cherry Chutney," Carina Monroe whispered, hiding her face behind the memorial program so no one could see that she was talking to herself. "Yellow roses. And Tanner."

She peered over the top of the program, pretending to fan her face. Well-dressed men and women were slowly filling the rows of white chairs arranged on the bright green lawn. The memorial was taking place outside because too many mourners were expected for the cemetery's chapel. Carina supposed she should be grateful that it was a perfect spring afternoon; rain would certainly have complicated things.

At least the burial was over: Carina didn't think she could bear to look at the casket for another second, a reminder not only of what she'd lost but also of the fact that she was now truly alone in the world.

Carina wondered if the lab was helping to foot the bill. Mountain Grove was the most beautiful cemetery in the area, and no expense had been spared here either: the chairs were covered with white slipcovers, potted lilies adorned each row, and floral arrangements overflowed the area around the platform. Discreet staff assisted people in finding seats, and white-shirted caterers worked efficiently to set up the long tables of refreshments that would be served following the service.

She scanned the people arriving, the staff members, even the vehicles lining the service drive that disappeared around the building. Good—no one seemed to be watching, not even the security detail assigned to keep an eye on her. So no one had heard her doing her daily appreciations, a habit she'd begun after her mother, Madelyn, died last June and her therapist suggested she list three things she was grateful for every day.

The therapist hadn't been particularly helpful, but maybe that was because Carina made a practice of lying to him. The biggest lie was that her mother's career had been so demanding that the two of them hadn't been close. Carina insisted that her life wasn't that different now that her mother was gone—she'd been taking care of herself since she was in grade school, she said, and going to live with Uncle Walter after Madelyn's death was just a change of scenery.

Besides, as Carina frequently reminded the therapist, Madelyn hadn't been especially maternal. She'd been reserved, not very affectionate, uncomfortable with intimacy— the exact opposite of nurturing. So, Carina insisted, she'd stopped depending on her mother long ago for emotional support.

It wasn't true, of course. Carina, who'd never known her father, couldn't recall a day in her life when she hadn't wished her mother were more available. But it was easier to pretend that everything was fine, and once Carina was committed to that version of the story, there didn't seem to be much point in being honest about anything else, so she simplified things further by telling the therapist what he seemed to want to hear: *I'm sleeping well, my appetite's good, I'm doing great in school.*

Yeah. Not so much.

But to Carina's surprise, some of the therapist's advice wasn't too bad. Like telling her to return to the track team right away; training did keep her sane. Seeing her friends never failed to cheer her up, even if she felt like she was sleepwalking through their get-togethers.

And then there were the appreciations. They seemed stupid at first, but just thinking of things to be grateful for and saying them out loud every day did make her feel better. Carina usually did them first thing in the morning, but today had been a mad dash to get ready for the memorial. This was the first chance she'd had to catch her breath, the first moment she'd been left by herself all day.

She wasn't sure if it was cheating, but one of her appreciations was always the same, ever since she'd met Tanner Sloan last September. He was the best thing to happen to Carina for as long as she could remember. The other two were kind of lame today, but what could you expect on the day you buried your last living relative? Besides, Carina truly did appreciate her manicure, the deep red polish called Black Cherry Chutney. And she was grateful for the bouquet of lilies and yellow roses that had arrived this morning, a gift from her best friends, Nikki and Emma.

She looked for them in the crowd; they had promised to come, along with most of the track team. She finally spotted them in line to be seated, far back behind the chairs, and resigned herself to not being able to talk to them until after the service. The security staff would never allow her to go sit with them. The two guards assigned to her, nearly identical men named Baxter and Meacham, had taken up posts at either end of her row, as though they were guarding a bomb rather than an orphaned high school girl.

Earlier in the day, when Uncle Walter had been laid to rest at the private graveside service, the security staff had had their work cut out for them keeping uninvited guests away from the cordoned-off area. But the memorial service was open to the public, and Baxter and Meacham were busy screening the crowd for suspicious characters. What constituted a suspicious character, Carina had no idea, but since her uncle had worked for the Calaveras National Laboratory on projects involving national security, the presence of armed guards was evidently a matter of course.

If Carina had had her choice, she wouldn't have a security detail, much less hundreds of people she didn't know, at her uncle's funeral. But she was glad Baxter was there. He'd begun working at the lab five years earlier, and he had always been kind to her. And when he was moved from the general security pool to head up the team working on Madelyn and Walter's project, he'd taken a special interest in Carina. He had gone above and beyond the call of duty, driving her to activities if Madelyn and Walter couldn't get away from work. Baxter was the one who came to get her when she caught the flu at school. He teased her about boys as though she were his kid sister, not his bosses' daughter/niece. At her mother's funeral, it had been Baxter who'd made sure Carina had a small pack of tissues for her purse. On her birthday, he'd sent a card; he'd signed it "The Team," but she recognized his handwriting. He'd even come to watch her compete at the state track championships last year.

Meacham, on the other hand, was all business. He hardly ever spoke unless it was into his little Bluetooth mike, and never, ever cracked a smile. He looked like all the other security guards employed by the Calaveras National Lab: fit, reasonably attractive men in their twenties and thirties. Dark suits, starched white shirts, sunglasses, buzz cuts—it was like they had all trained with the Secret Service.

Meacham and Baxter had been waiting when Carina and Sheila Boylston pulled up at the funeral home. Sheila Boylston was the guardian Uncle Walter had appointed in his will, and a longtime friend and colleague who'd worked with Madelyn and Walter for years. Sheila had shown up at Carina's school as soon as she'd heard the news about the accident, and by that night she'd moved Carina into her sterile condo with its sharp-angled furniture and echoing minimalist rooms.

Carina flashed back to the memory of arriving at her mother's funeral, when Walter had comforted her in the car. Sheila had tried to make Carina feel at home, and Carina knew she meant well, but there was no way she could lean on her for support the way she'd leaned on Walter then.

Madelyn Monroe's funeral hadn't been this well attended, but that was probably because her job at the lab hadn't been as high profile as Uncle Walter's. Their work had started to attract public attention only after her death. Her suicide had caused quite a stir for a while, especially since rumors always flew about the secret projects being conducted at the lab, but Carina knew that their research was far less exciting than it seemed. "Basically, we're building the modern K ration," Uncle Walter always said. Researching ways to optimize nutrition for the armed services might have been important work, but it was also dull.

Still, Walter was the head of their division, and he'd been interviewed on television half a dozen times in the last year because of a massive contract that was rumored to be in negotiations, one that would bring hundreds of jobs to the city of Martindale, California. Peace protestors and lobbyists from the capital were frequent presences at the lab, as were scientists visiting from all over the world, all of whom brought media attention. That explained the news crews milling around with their cameras at a barely respectful distance.

It was bad enough to have a security detail at your loved one's funeral; knowing it was going to be broadcast around the country was downright depressing. Carina checked her watch: still ten minutes to go. She pressed her hand to her forehead. She'd been feeling light-headed and feverish all morning but had chalked it up to the stress of the funeral and the delayed sense of loss and grief. But now her pulse was racing and a strange, jittery sensation had taken over her nervous system.

Maybe if she went to the restroom, splashed cold water on her face, she'd feel better. She scanned the people gathered at the front of the crowd and spotted Sheila standing with the minister and the mayor. When they had arrived for the memorial, Sheila told her at least twice to let her know if she needed anything, and not to go anywhere without telling her, but Carina couldn't catch her eye. She sighed—she was seventeen years old, not five, and perfectly capable of going to the bathroom by herself.

Still, when she got up and started to make her way down the row, Meacham hastened toward her, looking worried.

"Miss Monroe, is something wrong?" he asked, taking her arm so that they blocked the aisle. His grip was light, but Carina bet he could break bricks with that hand. She stared into his sunglasses, seeing only her own face reflected back, and tried a smile on him. Unlike Baxter, Meacham didn't fall for her smile; his expression—or lack of an expression—didn't change.

"Oh, hey, Meacham. I was just on my way to the ladies' room." She stared into his sunglasses, challenging him to look away.

"I'll be happy to accompany you."

"I'm not sure that's allowed," Carina said, her temper beginning to fray. "They usually don't let men in there."

This was getting ridiculous. At every event sponsored

by the Calaveras National Lab—even company picnics—you could spot men like Baxter and Meacham. The lab was surrounded by high-security electric fencing, even though it was disguised to look like iron scrollwork at both entrances, and there were two separate guard booths that you had to pass to gain admission. Carina had made a joke once that the second guy was there in case you shot the first guy, and Walter had looked startled and failed to laugh along with her.

Ordinarily, the security staff took pains to stay in the background, but today there were at least two dozen of them, and Carina had seen several of their vehicles—dark-windowed SUVs with the lab's parking sticker on the back window—parked close to the event.

Meacham didn't respond to her attempt at a joke, so Carina gave up and started down the aisle to the main building, threading her way through the guests while he trailed after her. She scanned the crowd for Baxter and found him at the other end of the row, his hands behind his back. He glanced over at her with a hint of a smile, and she gave him a covert little wave.

When they got to the restroom, Carina put her hand on the door and turned to face Meacham. "Seriously, Meacham, I think I can take it from here."

"I'll be right outside." He took off his sunglasses, revealing cool gray eyes, and leaned against the wall, focusing on the people walking up and down the corridor. He glared suspiciously at a man pushing a cart stacked with coffee cups.

"Hey, Meacham ..." Carina paused in the doorway, her

curiosity winning out. "Why are you following me around? No offense, but I can't believe there's much of a security risk. I mean, my uncle wasn't exactly a celebrity or anything."

Walter might have been high up in the lab's hierarchy, but at heart he was a geek, a guy with not one but two PhDs, from MIT and UCLA, who had trouble making conversation at parties but could talk for hours about DNA-binding proteins. He was usually dressed sloppily and had to be reminded to get haircuts, and he misplaced his car keys almost every day. He'd done pioneering work with viral genomes and lectured all over the world, but he couldn't name a single celebrity or popular television show. The lab had hired a coach to help him with his media appearances, but the man Carina would always remember had an awkward smile and wore wrinkled shirts, the kind of guy who could disappear in a crowd or even a packed elevator.

Meacham squinted at her, his mouth turning down in a faint frown. "His work was highly classified."

Carina rolled her eyes. Of course people paid attention to her uncle's project because of the jobs it would bring to the community, but she doubted that anyone cared very much about modifications to the diet of armed services members.

In the bathroom, two women were touching up their makeup at the sink. Carina thought she recognized one of them from some social function, and when she saw the woman's look of sympathy reflected in the mirror, she bolted into an empty stall rather than have to deal with making small talk. She'd had plenty of that already today, accepting the condolences of everyone who'd approached her at the graveside service. She'd have to grit her teeth and get through more socializing after the memorial, but at least Tanner and Nikki and Emma were out there somewhere, and they would be at her side the minute the official part of the program was over and they were allowed to mingle. Once she was with her friends, everything would be easier.

When Carina emerged from the stall, the bathroom was empty. She washed her hands and dabbed her face with a dampened paper towel. The feverish sensation hadn't faded; she didn't really feel ill, just sort of... hypersensitive. Her pulse was still racing, her nerves buzzed with electricity, and everything seemed magnified. Sounds were louder, colors brighter; she could make out the conversations of people many yards away.

She stood for a moment looking in the mirror, not yet ready to go back outside and deal with Meacham. She thought she looked okay, especially considering she'd cried most of the night, once she was alone in Sheila's guest room with the door locked. She'd expected her eyes to be puffy this morning, but they weren't—the facial she'd had yesterday must have worked wonders on her skin.

Sheila wasn't exactly a warm and fuzzy person herself, and Carina figured it was easier for her to book four hours of hair and beauty treatments at the most luxurious spa in town than to actually ask her about her feelings—but she appreciated the gesture. Besides, it was better than sitting around a strange apartment thinking about Walter and the life they'd shared, the life that had shattered overnight when his rental car hit an embankment on his way from the Houston airport to give a talk at Rice University.

Carina's long chestnut hair had been trimmed and accented with highlights. Her brows were shaped, and she'd had a steam facial and exfoliation, as well as a pedicure and gel manicure.

Before the salon visit, they'd gone to a boutique downtown, the kind where the clothes have no price tags and they offer you herbal tea or champagne while you shop. The saleslady had studied Carina and then brought her things to try on without ever asking her size. Carina had chosen a dress that she'd never have picked on her own but had to admit looked good on her: a deep shade of navy blue, close fitting but not tight, with a wide neckline that showed her collarbones and a skirt that flared out to swirl above her knees.

When the saleslady rang up the dress—and high-heeled navy sandals to go with it—Carina was shocked by the cost. But before she could protest, Sheila laid a hand on her arm and handed over her credit card.

"For Walter," she said. "Let's send him off in style."

Now Carina turned to check the back of her dress in the mirror, appreciating the smooth fabric, the way it draped over her hips. It was probably wrong to be thinking of Tanner at a time like this, but she was looking forward to him seeing her in the dress. Especially after last night.

Coloring at the memory, Carina took off the ring she had removed to wash her hands. It was the only jewelry she wore, a gift from her mother on her seventeenth birthday, a couple of months before she died. Carina didn't often wear it because it was bulky and tended to spin on her finger, but the large green stone looked perfect with the navy dress.

Green had been her mother's favorite color, and the jade was veined with several shades from pale celery to deep pine.

There was a knock at the door. "Miss Monroe? Everything okay?"

Meacham. Of course. Carina sighed before answering. "Just dealing with a feminine issue," she said maliciously. Maybe that would embarrass him enough to make him go away.

"I'll be right here," he said after only a brief hesitation. Okay, so maybe they covered that at secret agent school.

Carina picked up her ring and examined the stone, which was carved into a hexagon and polished to a bright shine. One of the prongs looked a little crooked, and Carina tested it with her fingernail.

It seemed to give, and Carina's heart sank. That was all she needed today, to lose the stone from the ring, but she had brought only a small handbag without a secure closure and she didn't want to risk storing the ring in the bag. Trying to decide whether it was safe to wear the ring, she slipped the tip of her polished fingernail under the prong, looking for damage along the small, sharp bit of white gold that held the stone in place.

As she brought it up close to her eye, she noticed that the prong wasn't like the others—it was hinged at the bottom, a minuscule clasp lifting away as she tugged at the tip. She caught her breath when it snapped backward and the stone popped out.

It didn't fall all the way out. Carina gingerly tapped the

stone. Solid: something was keeping it in place. Holding the ring under the fluorescent light, Carina looked underneath at the flat surface of the setting.

It wasn't entirely flat. Etched into the gold were characters of some sort . . . numbers. They were so tiny that Carina could barely make them out, but as she squinted, they came into focus. Two rows of numerals, with a few letters mixed in. There were fifteen or twenty characters in all.

"Miss Monroe? I'm going to need to come check on you if you don't come out now." Meacham sounded annoyed. Carina hastily pushed the stone back down, and it snapped into place. She slid it onto her finger just as the door to the ladies' room opened and Meacham stood in the entrance, glaring at her with suspicion.

"So sorry to keep you waiting," Carina said, forcing a smile. "Little wardrobe malfunction. But don't worry, I've got everything under control."

Pushing past Meacham before he could respond, she hurried back toward the crowd, which seemed to have doubled since she'd been gone. She waved at her friends, but they didn't see her. She scanned the people filling the seats and standing along the aisles and in the back, searching for Tanner, but there were easily a few hundred people assembled and she didn't see him anywhere. Baxter was hovering at the other end of her row, looking anxious.

She allowed Meacham to help her to her seat, giving him her best innocent look, eyes downcast. While she waited for the service to begin, she took a plain white envelope out of her purse for the third time since leaving the house, running her fingers over the smooth surface, tracing the letters of her name. She couldn't bear to read its contents yet, not here, not alone. She returned it to her purse and picked up the program from where she'd left it under her seat, and stared at her uncle's photograph. He was looking directly at the camera and laughing, wearing a suit and tie—a photograph that did not reflect the shy man she'd known and loved.

Carina concentrated on keeping her breathing slow and even. All around, the buzz of murmured conversations failed to cover up the fact that this was one of the loneliest days of her life.

CHAPTER TWO

Friday, 4:55 p.m.
12:58:06

Carina heard very little of the eloquent speeches during the service. The director of the laboratory spoke, as did several of the people Walter had worked closely with over the years. He hadn't had many friends—work was his life. Sheila spoke, and Carina tried to focus on her words, but her mind kept going back to the last few occasions she and Walter had really spent time together. He'd been especially distracted in recent months, staying late at work nearly every night, his thoughts a million miles away when he was at home. Carina was focused on other things too. There was her relationship with Tanner, her friends from school, and a part-time job at the mall over the holiday break. Once track season had begun, she'd had practice every night.

As the months passed, Walter worked longer and longer

hours, and they barely saw each other. Carina had noticed that something was different—okay, something was *wrong*. There, she admitted it, though doing so caused tears to well in her eyes. Something had been wrong with Walter, but he—like her mother—was not the sort to talk about his feelings, and Carina had been too preoccupied, too selfish, to ask him what it was.

Memories started surfacing, like the time he'd come home after two in the morning, and Carina happened to be in the kitchen getting a glass of water. He looked so exhausted and anxious as he set down his briefcase that Carina had finally asked him if he was feeling all right, and he'd produced a weak smile for her and said that it was nothing. So she'd let it drop, never mentioned it again.

Carina struggled not to cry, squeezing her elbows against her sides and curling her toes inside the expensive shoes, ignoring Sheila when she stepped away from the platform and walked down the aisle to their seats. She pretended to pay attention during the rest of the service, standing when everyone else stood, bowing her head when the pastor gave the final blessing. At last it was over, and people began to gather their things and make their way over to the refreshments.

"I'm going to go find my friends," Carina said, avoiding Sheila's eyes as she stood. She was already backing down the aisle, letting the crowd carry her along, but Sheila frowned.

"Can't it wait? This is your—"

"I'll be right back, I promise," Carina lied. She felt guilty— *This is your uncle's memorial service,* Sheila had been about to say, and Carina knew she had responsibilities: receiving condolences, talking to the pastor. But she needed her friends now. Nikki, who could always make her smile with her crazy antics, and Emma, who was quiet around people but had called twice a day since Walter died, just to check in. And Tanner, who could make everything a little better just by saying her name.

She started toward where she'd last seen her friends, but the crowd made it hard to see. By the time she spotted Emma's turquoise dress, they were practically outside the cordoned-off area, being hustled along by security staff. It looked like Nikki was trying to argue, but while Carina watched, one of the guards took her arm and forced her to keep walking.

"Carina." She whirled around to find Tanner coming toward her, almost knocking over chairs in his determination to reach her. He was hard to miss: six feet two, with the blond hair and cobalt-blue eyes that were the hallmarks of his Norwegian ancestry. Tanner cut his hair only when his mother insisted, and at the moment it was hanging over his forehead and curling over the collar of his oxford button-down. His tie was loosened and hung askew.

As he approached, she saw him notice her dress, her high heels, the makeup and highlighted hair, and her heart lifted a little. Wrapping his arms around her, Tanner held her close long enough to whisper in her ear: "I'm so sorry, Car. I tried to come sit with you, but they wouldn't let me. They're trying to get everyone out to the reception area. I almost had to tackle a guard to get past him."

Carina only nodded, not trusting herself to speak until she'd swallowed the lump in her throat. She was usually good at keeping her feelings under control, a skill that wasn't that hard to come by with a family like hers, but when she was with Tanner, all of her usual barriers evaporated.

She finally pulled away and gave him an uneven smile. "You're awfully hot."

"Uh . . . thanks?"

Carina blushed. "No, I mean, your *skin* seems hot. Feverish. Are you all right?"

"Actually, I feel like I'm coming down with something. I've had a headache all morning, like someone's trying to saw my skull in half. And yeah, I think I do have a fever." He held out his hand and Carina saw that it was trembling. "I'm definitely off my game."

"Oh no, I hope I didn't give it to you. I'm not feeling all that great myself." Which wasn't exactly true—she just felt *weird,* not bad.

"If you did, it was worth it," Tanner said with great sincerity, making Carina blush.

She was glad he was still thinking about last night, that it had been as unforgettable for him as it had for her. "I didn't mean—"

"I'm sorry, I shouldn't have said anything. I mean, not today, not when . . . you know. But, hey, it was a great way to swap germs," Tanner said. "That's all I'm saying. Intimate contact."

Carina's phone chimed a new text and she looked down, grateful for the distraction. It was Nikki, saying that they were sorry they hadn't been able to get past the guards after the service and that she'd call later. Carina put the phone back in her purse and gave Tanner a smile. "I had a wonderful time last night," she said sincerely.

The night before, Tanner had picked her up after she'd gotten home from the salon. The plan was to go out for dinner, but he'd surprised her by bringing a picnic basket and a stack of old blankets and driving to the empty parking lot at Martindale High School. The view from the roof of the main building was the best in town, if you were willing to scale the ladder extending from the fire escape. Few people knew about the ladder, or how to unlatch it; a senior on the track team had showed Carina last year.

The sunset had been spectacular, a sea of gold and pink and orange surrounding the bright descending globe. They watched until the sun disappeared behind the horizon, and the lights of town came on one by one until there was a blanket of gold below and a sky full of stars above. Tanner had asked her if she wanted to talk about Walter, and promised that he'd listen all night if that was what she needed.

But that wasn't what had happened. Because what Carina needed was a respite from the crushing grief and loss that now had returned to her life after her mother's suicide and her uncle's death. She needed to be held. She needed to be touched. And when things somehow ended up going further with Tanner than they'd ever gone before, she was the one who asked him not to stop. She was the one who knew in her heart that it was the right night to make love to him for the first time.

And she wasn't sorry. Tanner had made her feel cherished from the day they'd met last fall, at the climbing gym where they both worked out off-season. That day, she'd fallen and twisted her ankle and he'd gone to get ice, then insisted on driving her home. She only knew that he was a rich kid from the private school across town, not the type she usually dated.

But Tanner was different. For one thing, he was from a loud, boisterous family of four boys in which everyone talked at once. His two middle brothers tackled him, his littlest brother crawled all over him, and his parents said "I love you" every time he left the house, even if it was just to go for a run. He was sweet and demonstrative with her, and for a girl who had grown up never knowing her dad, whose mother had always seemed too busy for her, the attention was irresistible.

And they never ran out of things to talk about. They were both secret geeks: Tanner loved computers, and Carina had been hooked on math and puzzles ever since Uncle Walter had begun giving her simple problems to solve when she was little. They talked about the superhero movies they both liked, and on their second date, when conversation gave way to kissing and they never made it to the movie because they lost track of time, Carina realized something else about Tanner: he could make her feel things no one else could, make her want things she'd never known she wanted.

They'd come close to having sex before—very close—but it wasn't until last night that Carina couldn't stand to wait any longer. When it was over, Tanner kissed her eyelashes, the corners of her mouth, her hair, and told her she was everything to him. In fact, she was pretty sure he'd been about to say "I love you."

But that was the one thing she couldn't allow, and she'd stopped him with a kiss. The most important people in Carina's life—her mother and uncle—had never said "I love you," and now they were gone. If Carina let Tanner say the words out loud—if she ever said them herself—then she would let him matter more to her than she could bear. She knew that if she lost one more person she loved, it would be the end of her.

Lately, she was starting to worry that simply not saying "I love you" wasn't enough—she'd started to realize that love could grow even when you were determined not to let it. So now she had to be extra careful. Sex was just sex, she told herself, and she would stay in control by not letting it get to her head. If Tanner had been surprised, if he'd been disappointed, he didn't let on, and the moment had passed.

"Let's find somewhere private," Carina suggested.

Outside the roped-off area, people were getting drinks and food, talking softly as they wandered past the photo display of Uncle Walter. Carina guided Tanner to a stone bench facing an arbor covered with climbing roses. They sat with their backs to the crowd, Carina nestled into Tanner's arms.

"So, you got through the service," Tanner said. "The hardest part is over, right?"

"I don't know. I feel kind of numb."

"That's probably normal, given everything you've been through."

"Yeah ... but listen, things don't really seem that normal at all. Something strange happened. Before the service, I was in the bathroom, washing my hands, and I somehow snapped the stone off my mom's ring. And underneath ..."

She removed the ring and found the hinged prong, slipping her fingernail underneath as she had done before. The stone lifted, and she showed Tanner the writing beneath it.

Holding it up to his eyes, Tanner focused on the tiny numbers, not saying anything for a moment. Carina recognized the signs of his intent concentration: his right eyebrow lowered while he rubbed his chin with his knuckle. Tanner could lose track of everything around him when he was working on a problem, and his focus had paid off—he would be studying computer science at Berkeley in the fall, with one of the top programs in the country.

After a few minutes he shook his head. "I don't know, Carina ... I think this is your thing, since it has the alpha characters mixed in—it's a code, right?" He handed the ring back. "Your mom never told you about the stone?"

"No." Madelyn had said only that it had been in the family when she presented it to Carina. At the time, Carina couldn't help suspecting that her mother had actually forgotten to go shopping for a gift—it wouldn't be the first time—and had given her a piece that she didn't much care for herself. But Carina kept it in the carved walnut jewelry box that Uncle Walter had brought back for her from a trip to Mexico, and counted it among her most prized possessions, even if she rarely wore it. She had so little that belonged to her mother.

Carina stared at the characters, running her fingertips over the cool edges of the large green stone, thinking. Something about them was familiar. Ever since she was little, she'd had a sixth sense with numbers. In middle school she'd figured out the fundamentals of calculus from the advanced algebra problems her teacher gave her when she got bored.

Now, as she traced the hexagon, she noticed something odd about the alpha characters: there were only a few that repeated.

"This is hex format!" she exclaimed.

Tanner peered over her shoulder. "I think you're right," he said after a moment. "Can you translate—"

"Just give me a second," Carina said, getting a pen out of her purse. She turned the funeral program over—she wasn't planning to keep it; she didn't want a photograph of Walter that looked nothing like him. Quickly, she scrawled a conversion grid on the back of the program and translated the characters.

"That's an IP address!" Tanner exclaimed when she was finished. "I can't believe how fast you did that."

"I'm awesome that way," Carina said, trying to cover up the hitch in her voice.

Though she was gifted with anything mathematical, her confidence had been shaken when she didn't get into Berkeley. After her mother's death, her grades had plummeted, and she'd only recently been able to focus in school again. She had been accepted into Cal State Long Beach for next year, but it was four hundred miles away. Besides the fact that they had no cryptography program, it meant being separated from Tanner, something she didn't like to think about.

"I only wish I knew what this address means—and why it's on my mom's ring," she said, changing the subject.

"Calaveras Lab home page?" Tanner suggested, one eyebrow raised.

Carina slipped the ring back on her finger. She knew Tanner was joking about her mother's devotion to her job, but still . . . if her mother had been the tattoo type, she probably would have gotten the lab's logo—a graphic of overlapping sine curves—tattooed on her arm.

Madelyn had worked especially long hours at the lab in the months before she died. Carina almost never saw her. Carina's therapist had gently suggested that the depression leading to Madelyn's suicide might have been made worse by the narrowness of her life, the fact that it revolved around work and that she had no outside interests.

Looking back on her high school years before Tanner, Carina realized that she had been well on her way to becoming just like her mother and uncle, spending long hours on problems, fueling her passion for math and cryptography. On the track team, she pushed herself just as hard, and routinely won the long- and high-jump events. She sometimes skipped social events to stay home and study, something Nikki especially gave her a hard time about. Because Madelyn and Walter valued focus and drive, she worked hard to earn their admiration, trying to substitute it for their attention.

Then she'd met Tanner and realized that her life could contain more than work and study. She had applied to Berkeley because of their strong math program, but she'd also looked forward to being near Tanner during college. Now, though, the future stretched ahead like a giant question mark. For the moment, she had a place to live—Sheila said she was welcome to stay with her until she left for college—and there was some sort of trust fund that Uncle Walter left that would pay for her schooling and whatever else she needed. She was a little hazy on the details, but she knew the lawyers would figure it all out.

"We can check that address on my computer, if you want to come over," Tanner said. "I mean, if you can."

Carina felt her mood slip, the brief distraction of decoding the address already fading. "I'm supposed to stay at Sheila's tonight. I guess some people are coming over. Bringing food and all that."

After her mom's funeral, the casseroles kept coming to her uncle's house for several weeks. It was weird, the way people brought food when they didn't know what else to do. And scientists had to be among the worst at expressing emotion; many of them seemed to be at a loss for words when they showed up with their Tupperware containers full of lasagna and salads.

Almost a year ago, Carina had stood in the kitchen staring at the mounting pile of food on the counter, wishing she'd tried harder to be close to her mother. Maybe if she'd been more outgoing herself, the type of person who could chatter on about anything, or if they'd shared more interests—if Carina had asked her to take up tennis or yoga or go shopping once in a while—Madelyn would have opened up to her. Maybe if she'd simply pretended to need her mother more, for the kinds of talks other girls seemed to have with their moms, about boys and sex, she would have made it true. The problem was that Carina hadn't had any questions left after her mother gave her a stack of books on the subject of sexuality and reproduction.

"I understand," Tanner said, resting his chin gently on top of her head. "I'll be there, though, if you need me. Sitting by the phone."

Carina smiled against his smooth cotton shirt. "Yeah, I bet. I can just picture that."

Tanner was hardly the type to sit still. He'd taken up track in middle school when a gym teacher noticed him lapping the other kids during a class run and suggested he give it a try, as opposed to Carina, whose mother had always enrolled her in every after-school program she could find as a way of keeping Carina busy until she got home from work. After a season of cross-country, Tanner had tried the field events and discovered a talent for throwing things—shot, discus, and javelin—and he'd made the state finals for the last two years. He had the muscular build that resulted from intense training, a fact that girls never failed to appreciate.

"Okay. Maybe not sitting, but—I'm there for you, Car, if you need me."

That made Carina remember the letter. Now was the best opportunity she would have to read it with Tanner for company—and she definitely didn't want to read it alone. She glanced over at Sheila, who was glaring impatiently in their direction. She knew they didn't have much time.

"There is one thing," she said hurriedly, taking the envelope from her purse. "I found it this morning, when we went by the house so I could pick up a few things."

She'd wanted to get a handbag that matched the navy dress, and Sheila had waited in the car while she went inside. It had been so strange to be in the house she'd shared with Walter, for the first time in nearly a week. His presence still lingered, in the newspaper he'd left folded on the hall table, in the faint scent of the coffee he loved so much. Carina had hurried to get her things, overcome by all the memories. After grabbing her purse and a few changes of clothes, she noticed the recycling can in the hall and remembered that it was pickup day. She took the can so she could dump it in the bin and wheel the bin out to the curb on her way out.

A letter had been hidden under the can. The envelope bore her name in Uncle Walter's handwriting, apparently left there before his trip to Texas, before the accident. Carina knew immediately that he'd wanted her to find it; he'd hidden it there knowing that she never forgot to take out the trash and recycling.

When Carina discovered the letter, a wave of grief passed through her that was so strong she felt like she was going to break down on the spot. It was the last thing Uncle Walter gave to her, the last time he wrote her name, and suddenly all the feelings of love and loss that she'd been carefully suppressing for the last few days threatened to erupt. And that couldn't happen. She had to go back outside and get in the car with Sheila and make conversation like nothing was wrong. The idea of confiding in Sheila was too uncomfortable to consider. Carina was grateful to have a place to stay, but the truth was that she and Sheila had been little more than friendly acquaintances until tragedy had forced them together.

So she'd stuffed the letter into her purse for later.

"He must not have meant for you to find it right away," Tanner said. "Otherwise he would have left it out in the open."

"That's what I was thinking."

"You want to open it now? I'd understand if you wanted to wait until you were in private."

"This *is* private. As private as I need it to be, anyway."

Carina opened the envelope with care and pulled out a single page, typed and signed in Uncle Walter's careless, sloppy handwriting. A key fell out of the folded paper, a plain brass house key with no markings. Carina exchanged a look with Tanner, and they began to read.

```
Carina,

    With any luck I'll be back before
you even see this, but just in case,
I wanted to tell you two things.
```

First of all, if anything happens to
me, and I don't mean to worry you,
but just in case, you MUST be careful
around Sheila Boylston. Do not speak
to her about me. Try not to go anywhere
with her alone.

The second thing is that I'm so
glad you're in my life. I know you're
my niece, but I've come to think of
you like a daughter, and I'm proud of
everything you do and the person you
are growing up to be. Sorry, that was
probably a little mushy!

If you do get this letter and I am
gone, get to the address below as soon
as you can, and use this key. Do not
tell anyone where you are going. You'll
learn more when you get there.

I'm sorry that I wasn't able to talk
to you about this sooner, but something
has recently come up that makes this
critically important.

I am also sorry that I let things go
this far, that I have allowed you to
be endangered. I've been in denial. I
couldn't bring myself to believe that
someone I trusted deeply had betrayed
me. My work has been my life, Carina,
but in the end my pride and ambition
caused me to make some terrible
mistakes.

If I do return, as soon as I
get back I will work out a new

guardianship arrangement. I don't mean to worry you needlessly, so if you find this before I come home, just set it aside and I'll explain more later.

> Be good while I'm gone,
> Your Uncle W
>
> 220 Gordon Place
> Apartment 2E
> (Between Stockton & Powell)

The paper trembled in Carina's hand, and she realized that she had stopped breathing somewhere after the first few sentences.

"Holy shit," Tanner said.

"I don't ..."

Carina scanned the letter a second time, trying to comprehend Walter's message. But when she got to the bottom she still didn't understand. He was insistent that she stay away from Sheila Boylston—but why? Sheila and Walter had worked together for years, along with Madelyn. They'd written several papers together that had appeared in scientific journals, and submitted grant requests and research proposals. When Carina was younger she'd wondered if Sheila and Uncle Walter would get married someday, until she realized that each of them was essentially married to their job.

Sheila had been perfectly kind ever since they'd gotten the terrible news. Granted, she hadn't offered much in the way of comfort, at least not the hugging-and-hot-cocoa vari-ety, but like Carina's mother, Sheila had never been a warm, fuzzy person. She'd given Carina a room, food, bought her clothes, and even taken her to the spa. There really wasn't much more she could have done, given that she was dealing with her own grief as well as planning the memorial and funeral.

Uncle Walter had to have been mistaken about whatever he'd been worried about. Maybe they'd had an argument, or a misunderstanding, or—or—

"That's not like your uncle at all," Tanner said uneasily. "He's the most chill dad I know. I mean ..." He looked em-barrassed by his mistake.

"No, it's okay," Carina said, covering his hand with her own. "He *was* like my dad. I just wonder why he didn't talk to me about this instead of leaving a note."

"My guess is he was hoping he could wait to talk to you when he got back, and he didn't want to scare you before he left. And also ..." Tanner hesitated.

"What?"

"Well, it seems pretty paranoid, but I mean, if he was *really* worried, he might have been concerned that the house was bugged somehow. Listen, Carina ..."

"Just say it," she said, trying to ignore the dizzy rush of fear Tanner's words were causing.

"Well, are you sure this is his signature? His handwriting?"

Carina examined the letter and envelope carefully. It cer-tainly looked like Walter's blocky handwriting, his unintelli-gible signature. "I mean, yeah, I'm almost positive."

"So . . . that's good." But he looked doubtful.

"Tell me. Whatever you're thinking, Tanner, tell me."

"Just that it could be a fake. If someone had a copy of his writing, they could conceivably fool anyone who wasn't an expert."

"Why? Why would anyone go to that kind of trouble? I mean, seriously, Tanner, that would be—that would mean Uncle Walter had been killed on purpose, *and* someone didn't want me to trust Sheila, *and* they broke into our house and knew what day the recycling gets picked up—and left me this *key—*"

"Yeah, I get it, it's not very likely. But then again, neither is the idea that your uncle is tied up in some sort of . . . I don't know, black-ops thing."

"Black-ops?"

Tanner looked embarrassed. "Sorry, I don't know what to call it. I don't exactly have experience with this sort of thing. Listen—are you sure your uncle was working only on that nutrition project?"

"Well, yeah." His team had been working on it for several years, refining various kinds of proteins, trying to optimize delivery and packaging for portability in various environments and conditions. Walter hadn't talked about the project much, saying he knew how boring the topic was to most people.

Unless . . .

Unless he made the whole thing up. Because he was secretly working on something else.

"Because," Tanner said carefully, as if he knew what she

was thinking, "if he *was* working on something classified, and Sheila, I don't know, wasn't supposed to know—"

"But that doesn't make any sense. They worked *together.* They always did. My mom too."

Someone approached their bench, walking purposefully from the direction of the mourners, and Carina groaned. "Just what we need—Meacham."

"Who?"

"One of the security guys who was sitting with me and Sheila? Baxter's cool, but this guy—I don't know, he's got an overdeveloped sense of power or something. Listen—will you hang on to this? I'd just feel better about it in case he wants to go through my purse." She pressed the folded letter and key into Tanner's hand.

"Sure, only I've never really heard of anyone being searched at a memorial service," Tanner said, slipping the envelope into his pocket, covering the motion by shifting toward her.

"I'm serious, Tanner, these guys have been all over me. Hi," she added coldly as Meacham arrived in front of them.

"Miss Monroe, Ms. Boylston asked me to have you join her." The man barely spared a glance at Tanner.

"Huh. Well, seeing as I'm in the middle of a conversation with my friend right now, that's not really convenient." Carina held Meacham's gaze, even though a prickle of unease traveled down her spine. There . . . under his jacket. Shoulder holster, right? Which meant a gun. Which she'd always suspected, but now it seemed to imply that whatever he asked her to do was more than a friendly suggestion. Not that he'd ever use it on her, she knew, but it was hard to imagine saying no to a guy who was armed.

"Perhaps you could talk to your friend another time."

"Hey." Tanner got up and stepped between Carina and Meacham. "Over here? Yeah. *Me.* I'm the one she's having the conversation with, and if she says she isn't finished, then I guess she isn't finished."

Meacham turned his head a fraction of an inch to stare—sunglasses and all—into Tanner's eyes. They were about the same height, and the security guard matched Tanner's solid build from the broad shoulders to the muscular neck, but he didn't appear the least bit intimidated. "This really doesn't concern you," he muttered softly. "How about you go read a comic book or something."

"Leave him alone," Carina said, getting to her feet. She grabbed Meacham's arm, intending only to draw his attention away from Tanner.

And a funny thing happened. Strange funny ... and maybe a bit comical too, because somehow she pulled his arm a lot harder than she meant to, and he ended up tripping over his own feet. He stumbled as she leapt out of the way, and as he regained his footing his hand went to the inside of his jacket and suddenly he was crouched down in a shooter's stance with a gun in his hand.

"Are you out of your mind?" Tanner snapped, pulling Carina backward against him.

"What are you doing?" she demanded as Meacham appeared to think twice and quickly, almost sheepishly, stowed his gun. Whatever she'd done, it had unsettled him—and left her feeling plenty unsettled as well. The almost electric surge of energy that had accompanied her actions had not entirely subsided, and her nerves felt like vibrating guitar strings.

The feeling had to be caused by some sort of extreme adrenaline rush. She had eaten only a protein bar for breakfast, and it had been a very emotional morning; plus she'd been sitting still for too long. All of which should have made her *less* responsive, less alert, and certainly didn't explain her move on Meacham. He was a trained professional. How she'd managed to outmaneuver him—without even trying— was a mystery.

"Hey, hey, what's going on?" Baxter was jogging over, his hand on his earpiece. Meacham scowled, dusting himself off.

"Nothing," Carina said hastily, wondering if Baxter had seen the way she'd made his partner stumble. She gave him a smile that was meant to be reassuring. "A misunderstanding."

Baxter's expression softened. "Okay, Miss Monroe. Look, I know this is"—he cleared his throat before continuing, glaring at Meacham—"a hard day for you, and if there's anything we can do to make it go easier—"

"Maybe you could just keep Meacham company for a few minutes," she said, grabbing Tanner's hand and dragging him away, around the stone bench to the path that led farther into the gardens. She doubted it would be that simple, but she had to try. "We're going to go talk. Okay? I'll come find Sheila when we're done."

"Well, what do you know," said a familiar voice behind her. "I can save you the effort."

Carina whirled around and found Sheila standing with her arms crossed a few steps down the cobblestone path. Her mouth was set in a grim line. Apparently she'd recovered from her grief and moved straight to fury.

CHAPTER THREE

Friday, 5:37 p.m.
12:16:11

Carina moved closer to Tanner and gripped his hand tightly. "I told Meacham that I needed to finish talking to Tanner."

"And I wish there were time," Sheila said smoothly, quickly rearranging her features into the bland expression she usually wore. "But unfortunately, something has come up that requires you and me to go straight back to my house. Alone."

"Why, did you leave the oven on?" Carina said, not bothering to hide her sarcasm.

She had a smart-ass side that came out when she was stressed. It was something she'd been working on controlling, and more than once she'd had to apologize to Uncle Walter for something said in the heat of the moment. He had been very understanding. Sheila didn't look like she intended to be. Carina thought she saw Baxter trying to cover up a grin.

"No, the matter is of a far graver nature. As soon as we are *alone* I'll fill you in." She glared at Tanner, who scowled back.

"Actually, I'm not going anywhere without Tanner," Carina said as evenly as she could manage. "He's my boyfriend and I need him today. I just lost my *uncle,* in case you forgot."

Sheila looked like she was going to snap back, but instead she clamped her mouth shut and exhaled hard. So subtly that Carina thought she might have imagined it, Sheila made a small motion with her hand, and Meacham edged closer, circling around so that he was positioned between them and the thinning crowd.

"All right. In that case, *Tanner* is welcome to come back to the house with you for a while, but I really do need to speak to you in private for a moment. Tanner, you don't mind, do you? Carina and I will be right under that tree." She pointed at a flowering tree that shaded the path. "I promise we won't go anywhere without you."

Carina exchanged a glance with Tanner and let go of his hand. As she followed Sheila to the tree several yards away, she wondered if it was possible that this new and combative side of her guardian could merely be the result of the stress she'd been under—or if there really was something to her uncle's suspicions. Perhaps Walter and Sheila had had a fight before he died, and if Walter had lived they might have eventually patched things up, come to a new understanding.

There was no way to know now, and Carina had to decide whom to trust—and fast.

When they were under the tree, Sheila turned to face Carina with a grim expression.

"There are things you don't know about the project your uncle and I have been working on," she said before Carina could speak. "The situation isn't what it appears to be. Walter made some . . . unfortunate errors in judgment recently."

Her tone—accusatory and grating—set Carina's teeth on edge. Any desire she had to be fair, to give Sheila the benefit of the doubt, evaporated.

"Oh really? How would you even know that?"

Sheila blinked and Carina could see the effort she was making to keep her temper in check. "Walter and I worked together before you could talk, Carina."

"If anything was going on, I think I'd know, considering that I've been *living with him* for the past year."

"You have no idea what we were working on."

"Sure I do—your *nutritional research*, right?" Carina didn't bother to keep the skepticism out of her voice. "Only that's not really what you guys were doing at all, was it?"

Sheila stared at Carina for a moment, narrowing her eyes. Finally she took a step closer, leaving only inches between them. Up close, Carina could see the faint lines between her eyebrows and bracketing her mouth. Carina had always thought Sheila was attractive for her age, if you liked thin, wound-tight women, but up close her eyes had a hardness to them and her smile was forced.

"All right," she said softly. "All right. So this is how we're going to do this. I didn't want to risk tarnishing your uncle's memory in any way, but you aren't giving me a choice. You're right—our research was much more . . . shall we say, *far reaching* than you were aware of. Classified, in fact, so at least you don't need to be angry at your mom or your uncle for not telling you about it, because they were legally prevented from discussing it with you."

It stung to know her mother had kept secrets from her. Carina supposed she shouldn't be too surprised—she'd accepted long ago that her relationship with her mother was more distant than she would have liked. But this meant there had never been an adult in her life, not a single one, who had always been honest with her.

Still, she wasn't about to give Sheila the satisfaction of seeing her pain. She fixed a cold expression on her face and glared back. "And I should believe you . . . why?"

The corner of Sheila's eye twitched. "How about this— because you're in danger, serious danger, and I can keep you safe?"

Carina laughed bitterly. "Danger, really? Is that why Meacham won't even let me go to the bathroom by myself? Are you afraid bad guys are going to parachute into the stall and torture me until I tell them what Walter was working on? Oh, wait—it was *classified*, so there's no way I'd know anything about it anyway—right?"

"You need to shut up and listen," Sheila snapped. Out of the corner of her eye, Carina saw Tanner edging closer, Meacham close on his heels. "The press is reporting that your uncle died in a random auto accident on the way from the Houston airport. That's not entirely true. That embankment he crashed into? Two vehicles with bogus license plates forced him off the road. He couldn't have avoided the collision, and since he'd been trying to outrun them, he was going close to eighty miles an hour when he died."

Carina struggled not to blink. "I don't believe you."

"Believe *this:* those cars were driven by members of one of the most violent gangs operating in the Republic of Albania. They were after Walter because of some specialized research he was supposed to give them. Which, by the way, has nothing to do with nutrition and everything to do with enhancing battlefield performance. The Albanian mafia intends to use our work to fight a crackdown on cocaine trafficking by the government. If they are successful, many, many innocent people will die." Sheila sighed. "That technology we developed was meant for our own army, needless to say. Your uncle was a brilliant man—too bad he was so hardheaded."

"Uncle Walter would never get involved with anything like what you're saying," Carina said, outraged. "He was—" She struggled to find the words to describe him: brilliant, and passionate about his work, but he could also be funny, and on the rare occasions when he took a break from his job, he was kind and generous with her. In some ways, he'd been more of a parent to her than her own mother had been. She could no more imagine him cheating on anything than she could imagine him singing on *American Idol*.

"He was human." Sheila shrugged. "He made mistakes. For whatever reason, the Albanians thought they had made a deal with him, but he didn't actually hand over the research like he was supposed to. That's why he was killed. They made an example out of him. Now, unfortunately, our intelligence suggests that his contacts believe *you* have access to the data."

"Me? Why would they think that?"

"You were close to him," Sheila said.

"That's crazy. He never told me *anything*."

"Closer than anyone else," Sheila amended. "He told several people that you were his protégée. Before he made his last trip, Walter wiped his lab's servers of all his files, and changed all his passwords."

"What's going on?" Tanner demanded, putting his arm protectively around Carina. "Is she threatening you?"

"I'm trying to save her life," Sheila said. "If you try to get involved, you'll just endanger her further."

"She says some Albanian gang was after Uncle Walter to get at his research, but he hid it all before they killed him. And that now they're trying to find me because they think I have it."

"That's crazy," Tanner said. "They'd have a dozen different layers of data security at a place like Calaveras Lab. There's no way Mr. Monroe would have been able to single-handedly take it all down."

"Aren't you the clever one," Sheila snapped, glaring down her nose at Tanner. "You must belong to the computer club at school. A regular *prodigy*."

"I'd have to belong to the idiot club to believe that high-security government contract data isn't routinely encrypted and backed up."

"Indeed. But what you're not taking into account is Walter's private work. Technically, the lab owns anything developed by Walter even off-premises, but he seems to have been adept at blurring the lines. There were ... *elements* ... of our project that Walter alone had access to."

"So you're saying that my uncle had his own thing going on, something outside your supersecret 'battlefield enhancement' project, and *that's* what he was killed for?" Carina demanded. "That's what they think I have? What exactly is it, anyway? Some kind of extreme energy drink? Rock star in a pill?" There was that smart-ass side again, the one she couldn't contain when she was angry.

Sheila's grim expression turned even more scornful. "You don't need to worry about the details. All you need to know is that we have access to communications suggesting the Albanians believe Walter gave key information to you. The reason Baxter and Meacham have been so attentive today is that they are trying to keep you safe." She raised an eyebrow. "You might actually want to try being grateful."

"Grateful?" Carina said incredulously. "If you knew all this, if these Albanians are as big a threat as you say they are, then you practically got Walter killed yourself."

"Carina!" Sheila snapped. "You don't know what you're talking about. You have no idea how ruthless they can be. If they want you—and trust me, they do—then they're just waiting for the opportunity."

"If we were in so much danger, why didn't you say anything about it sooner?"

"I didn't think ..." Sheila shook her head impatiently. "I don't have time to explain. New information has come to light, and you can bet they have people on the ground close by, watching us even now—"

"I don't believe her," Tanner said, not bothering to lower his voice, never taking his eyes off Sheila. Meacham had a hand on his shoulder, and Tanner was trying to shrug him off without attracting the attention of the people who were wandering close to the gardens.

Carina didn't believe her either. Walter couldn't have been killed over something as simple as a performance-enhancing drug. Something else was going on, and she was beginning to feel certain that Sheila was at the center of it.

"Give me ten minutes to say goodbye to Tanner," she hedged. "Alone."

Sheila glanced impatiently at her watch. "You've got your priorities all mixed up," she said. "Your boyfriend should be the *last* thing on your mind. At least until we get this nailed down. In a few days' time the authorities should have the men who killed Walter in custody, and you can quit worrying about them. Until then, I highly suggest you let the grown-ups do what they're paid to do."

If it weren't for that final dig, that last bit of condescension, Carina might have agreed. But Sheila had been treating her rudely all day, snapping at her to hurry in the morning, and again when she was taking too long to walk to her seat. Gone was the solicitous kindness she usually showed Carina, the almost insistent generosity she'd exhibited at the salon. In its place was a cold efficiency that made Carina's skin crawl.

"Ten minutes," she repeated.

"It's okay, Ms. Boylston," Baxter said. "They're just kids. Give them a few minutes."

That earned Baxter a scowl, but Sheila reluctantly nodded, and Meacham let go of Tanner's shoulder. Carina took his hand and they practically jogged down the path until she was certain they were out of earshot.

"I'm sorry," she murmured to Tanner. "I can't believe I got you into this."

He pulled her closer. "This is really weird," he whispered against her ear, "and try not to react, but that guy Meacham showed me his gun. When you were talking to Sheila. Like, if I tried to mess with you he wasn't afraid to use it on me."

"Are you sure he wasn't just trying to intimidate you?"

"Uh, yeah. It's hard to misinterpret when a guy holds his jacket open and points to his holster, you know?"

"But Sheila said . . ." Sheila had said Meacham and Baxter were supposed to be protecting her, and presumably not just from the Albanian mafia. Was it possible he considered Tanner a threat?

And if she was to leave with Sheila—what guarantee did she have that Meacham wouldn't do something to Tanner the minute they were out of sight?

"This is so messed up," she said. "I wish we could just go somewhere, the two of us, and figure this out."

"Your uncle said to stay away from her. Do you trust her?"

Carina considered; it didn't take long at all for her to come up with an answer. "Yesterday I would have said yes.

Today? I don't know who to trust. But I certainly trust my uncle more."

"So come with me. Just us, we'll go somewhere alone and figure out your next move."

"Now, you mean? There's no way they'll let us."

"I don't know about that. It's the middle of a memorial service, and there's, like, half a dozen news crews here. Even those guys wouldn't risk making a scene that will end up on the Internet or TV."

Carina turned over the possibility in her mind. She had the key—and Walter's instructions to go straight to the address in his note. Whatever waited for them there, was it any riskier than staying here?

"Look over behind me, to your right," Tanner said. "Don't let them see you doing it, but ... there's a little road that goes around the Dumpsters. I'm pretty sure that's a service drive. We go that way, get a head start, there's no way they'll catch us before we get outside."

Carina calculated the distance to the wall that ringed the cemetery. If Tanner was right, there would be a break in the wall, just around the corner, for delivery trucks. If he was wrong ...

Well, he couldn't be wrong. That was all there was to it—because what he proposed was better than trusting Sheila.

"All right," she breathed against his neck, hoping Tanner looked convincingly like a guy consoling his distraught girlfriend. She felt his muscles tense under his shirt.

"On three, okay?" he said softly, and she subtly shifted

her stance, finding purchase on the gravel, wishing she weren't wearing such ridiculously high heels.

"One ... two ..."

When Tanner got to three she ran harder than she'd ever run in her life, ignoring the shooting pains in her feet from the shoes, narrowing her focus to a single thought: *Get away*.

CHAPTER FOUR

Friday, 6:10 p.m.
11:49:34

Before Carina had gone three strides, Sheila started yelling.

If Carina had been holding on to any hope that Sheila really did care about her welfare, that she was merely a dedicated scientist with a few paranoid notions, those hopes came crashing down when she heard the fury in her voice.

"Baxter, Meacham! *Go!* Stop them!"

Meacham grunted with exertion as he chased them, hindered by his close-fitting designer suit. Carina held tightly to Tanner's hand for balance as she ran, terrified of coming down wrong on her high heels and twisting her ankle. But the shoes didn't seem to be slowing her down at all. In fact, the strange jittery buzz she'd been feeling all day had roared to life, swelling to a crescendo in her ears, energy flowing through her body as though someone had flipped a switch. Tanner seemed to feel it too. He wasn't even breathing hard as they leapt over a cart loaded with folding chairs rather than swerve around it. Carina, who held a school record in the high jump, couldn't have done any better.

As they rounded the corner, Carina felt a surge of relief to see that the wall opened onto the street that ran along the south side of the cemetery. The tall, ornate gate was open, and a man pushing a handcart piled high with boxes was coming through.

"Excuse us!" Tanner shouted as the startled man hesitated in the opening. Carina swerved around the cart, unable to attempt the jump in her shoes, while Tanner headed straight for it. This time he didn't quite clear the tall boxes, hitting the top one with his foot; it fell to the ground, spilling small flowerpots that rolled in every direction behind them.

After she and Tanner passed through the gate, Carina pulled it shut with a clang, and the latch fell into place. She heard frustrated cursing behind them as their pursuers tripped over the flowerpots.

"This way!" Tanner shouted, running down the grassy median between lanes of traffic.

"Wait—"

Carina paused long enough to yank off her shoes and discard them on the ground. Then she was running barefoot, her feet sinking into the soft grass, her lungs filling with air as her arms and legs moved in tandem. When they reached the end of the block, she barely even felt the pavement beneath her feet, and she was sprinting faster than she ever had. Was her speed the result of terror? Adrenaline? Tanner was keeping up effortlessly—was he experiencing the same thing?

After another block they turned down an alley behind a row of bungalows, little square detached garages lined up on either side. When they came to a garage with its door open, the interior crammed with boxes and bikes and sports equipment, Carina had an idea. She swerved into the garage, praying that it was unoccupied, with Tanner right behind her.

Carina frantically scanned the wall for the button to close the garage door and slapped it hard. The door began to close, casting them gradually into darkness. When it groaned to a halt, the only light came from a grimy window facing the house. Through it, Carina could see a heavyset, sweating man mowing his back lawn with a push mower, sending up a spray of cut grass.

He'd only done a third of the backyard. If she and Tanner were lucky, they had a little time. Tanner was standing up against the garage door, his face pressed to its surface.

"What are you doing?" Carina whispered.

"There's a crack. I can see—wait—"

Carina held her breath until he spoke again. She stayed as still as she could, but her left eye was twitching. She rubbed it and it stopped immediately.

"He just passed by," Tanner said softly. "Meacham. And, Car—he had his gun out."

A chill ran through Carina. Would the man really shoot them? Or was the gun just to scare them into coming along?

She couldn't imagine that Sheila would actually risk killing anyone, no matter what the truth was about Walter, the gangsters, and the mysterious research.

She remembered something Sheila had said: *Our intelligence suggests that his contacts believe you have access to the data.*

If that was true . . . was it possible that Sheila actually believed that Carina had something valuable? Something Walter had given her, a way to access his private data? Sheila had said he had blocked access to his work the week before his trip: maybe he had actually been hiding the information from *her*?

Carina frantically racked her brain, trying to remember if Walter had given her anything that might contain whatever it was that Sheila wanted. They'd had breakfast together on the day before he'd left for Houston, oatmeal for Walter and a protein bar and a banana for Carina, as always. He'd brought a pizza home that night, after picking up the dry cleaning. Carina had been the one to bring in the mail, and there hadn't been anything unusual, just a couple of bills and some junk mail. Walter had gone to bed by ten since he had an early flight.

Nothing unusual at all. At some point, Walter must have hidden the letter under the recycling can in the hall. But if he'd left her anything else, she had missed it. And this wasn't the time to worry about it.

"We have to keep moving," Carina said. "Baxter and Meacham are both out there, and Sheila—"

Depending on how determined Sheila was to find her, there could be others. How many security agents had she seen at the edges of the crowd? A dozen? More? If they all worked for Calaveras, and if Sheila had the authority to order them around, the alley outside their hiding place could soon be crawling with people looking for them.

Baxter had always been kind to her, but Carina knew he wouldn't defy Sheila. She was his boss, and besides, he was a professional to the core. He wouldn't turn away from the job he was paid to do just to help her.

Tanner moved around the edge of the garage, pushing boxes out of the way. "There's a bike ... only one, though. Oh, flat tire. Don't suppose a Jet Ski will do us much good—"

"Tanner, my biggest problem is *shoes*," Carina said.

"Why didn't you say so?"

Near the door leading to the backyard was a rack containing ski boots, gardening clogs, and old sneakers. Tanner rifled through it, knocking over half a dozen shoes in his hurry. "How about these?"

He held up a pair of women's golf shoes with fringed tops. Carina grabbed them and tugged at the laces. "A little big," she said, jamming one on her right foot. "But I can tie them tight and—"

"You'd better hurry," Tanner said urgently. "The lawn mower man's— Oh, shit, I think he must be out of gas, he's coming over here—"

Carina yanked on the second shoe and fumbled with the laces. "I'm ready," she said just as Tanner hit the garage door opener. He grabbed her arm and they dove for the door, crouching low as it slowly creaked open, the man coming toward them.

"Hey, what the hell are you doing?" he shouted, but Tanner and Carina were already out.

"To the right!" Carina said. Coming down the alley at a run was Meacham, closely followed by Baxter and a third man who wasn't making any effort to hide the fact that he was talking into a radio as he jogged along. Carina recognized the Calaveras Lab's silver-and-red logo stitched on his jacket as he spotted her and veered toward them.

"This way," Tanner said, pulling Carina with him. They raced through the backyard behind the garage where they'd been hiding, through the lazy spray of a sprinkler, around a pair of little kids playing on a plastic slide.

"Gate ahead," Carina yelled without slowing. "Gonna jump it—"

The wooden gate was set into a fence, at least four and a half feet tall, that circled the yard. There was a latch, but if Carina took the time to unhook it, their pursuers would use those critical seconds to catch up. She hit the gate without slowing down, placing her hands over the tops of the boards, then jackknifing her body up and over, the way she'd practiced on the vault a hundred times before. The tops of her thighs scraped against the rough edge of the wood, but then her feet struck ground on the other side—a perfect landing.

She dashed out of the way just in time to avoid being crushed by Tanner, who'd hit the gate right after her. He didn't nail the landing as well as she had, coming down heavily and nearly falling before righting his balance. She waited to make sure he was unhurt; then they both took off running down the street as someone slammed into the gate.

Their pursuers apparently lacked the dexterity and strength to clear the gate the way she and Tanner had. She heard cursing and shots fired. Something whizzed by her ear.

"Tanner, watch out!" she screamed, but he was one step ahead of her, grabbing her hand and pulling her abruptly toward the cars parked along the edge of the street. She couldn't believe the security men were shooting—were they really trying to *kill* them? Hadn't Sheila said that she wanted to *protect* Carina?

She looked over her shoulder, despite knowing it would slow her down. There—there was Baxter, running in front of Meacham, pushing him out of the way. It might have been accidental—but from where Carina stood, it sure didn't look like it.

Was Baxter trying to protect her?

"Stay low!" Tanner called as they raced for the cover of the cars.

Something struck her upper arm. "Ow!" She slammed her hand over her biceps and touched a barbed piece of plastic. A *dart*? "Tanner, I've been—"

"Two blocks to the BART station," Tanner yelled. "Inbound train's coming!"

Carina looked where he was pointing. Rising over the street, the elevated tracks ran through downtown Martindale, carrying commuters the thirty miles across the mountains and the bay, and into San Francisco. And there, in the distance, was the train, its headlights winking as it approached.

If she really had been shot, Carina was just going to have to deal with it after she got on that train.

As she plowed forward, her vision began to swim in front of her. A strange, buckling sensation rippled through her muscles, and she stumbled. But Tanner didn't let go. The borrowed shoes hurt her feet, the leather rubbing against her toes and the backs of her heels. She ignored the pain and focused all her effort on not falling.

Forward ... just keep moving forward, one foot in front of the other. Again. Again. It was like when she used to run the 800-meter in middle school. Carina wasn't cut out for the event, but she'd given it her all, even as the other girls surged past her. She never placed in a single race, and more often than not she came in last, but she didn't stop trying. Each time, she hoped that her mother would come to the meet, that she would leave work early like she was always promising to do and stand in the bleachers with the other parents, watching her run, cheering her on.

That possibility kept her going through an entire losing season, before the coach finally decided to let her compete in the field events. It was just a matter of narrowing your attention until all that was left was the next step, and the next, until you hit the finish line and could collapse. Pain meant nothing; the raw scrape of air in your lungs meant nothing— that was what Carina had trained herself to believe as she surged toward the finish that would never be good enough.

The turnstile was in sight. Tanner dug into his wallet for his transit card and slid it through. "Go!" he shouted, waiting for her to pass. She let her momentum carry her, the metal bars sliding out of the way. But her legs felt wrong. Her foot flopped down at a strange angle, and this time, without Tanner to catch her, she couldn't recover. She fell hard on her hip, feeling the cold concrete scrape her skin as a startled woman jumped out of the way.

Tanner was through the turnstile now, and he took her hand and pulled her up. "Son, is she okay?" an old man asked, but they were already on the move. The train had arrived, and they raced for the escalator, Tanner practically carrying her.

"Too many people," Tanner panted as a crowd raced to make the train. "We'll never make it on the escalator. We have to use the stairs."

"I . . . can't," Carina gasped. Her vision had worsened; now she was seeing black spots, and the edge of the hand-rail seemed to waver in front of her.

And then she was airborne. Tanner had picked her up and thrown her over his shoulder, grunting as he took the stairs two at a time. Carina felt the blood rush to her face, watching the stairs pass below, her body limp and her muscles useless.

The train doors were starting to close as Tanner burst through them. He staggered to an empty seat and fell heavily into it, holding Carina in his arms. The last thing she felt before she lost consciousness was the train starting to move.

CHAPTER FIVE

Friday, 7:25 p.m.
10:34:22

"Come on, Car, wake up."

A gentle hand on her face. Tanner's voice. Something pressing against her leg.

Carina blinked, a wave of nausea passing through her as the scene around them swam and wobbled until it finally settled. Her eye was twitching again, like before, but this time it was several seconds before it passed and she was able to look around.

A train car. Fairly crowded. The thing pressing into her leg was the backpack belonging to the bored-looking man next to her. A guy in front of them was rocking out to the music from his earbuds. Carina could hear its harsh, tinny beat above the noise of the train.

She wiggled her fingers experimentally. They seemed

to work okay. She lifted her arms, shuffled her feet, and—once she was sure she wasn't paralyzed—straightened up in her seat. Her purse was nowhere to be seen; she must have dropped it at some point as they ran. She'd been leaning against Tanner, which was nice ... but as her mind cleared, her last few lucid moments came back to her.

The garage. The guys chasing them. Shooting at them.

"Hey!" she exclaimed, slapping a hand to her biceps. She could still feel the faint sting where the dart had entered her skin, but there was barely a mark, just a red dot.

Tanner unfolded his hand, showing her the dart lying on his palm. It was tiny, a tube with fringed plastic at one end and a wickedly sharp needle embedded in the other.

"Careful with that," Carina said.

"Yeah, don't worry. I just kept it because I thought—I don't know, maybe there's some way to have it tested and figure out what was in it."

"Something that knocked me out, obviously."

"Unless it was just my natural animal magnetism. Women faint around me all the time," Tanner said, attempting a smile as he jammed the dart into his pocket.

"How long was I out?" Carina said, struggling to her feet to look out the window.

Tanner shot out a hand to steady her. "Hey, hey, careful there."

"No, there's no time." She saw the Walnut Creek Medical Center whizzing by outside. "We're in Walnut Creek already. How long was it? Ten minutes?"

"Maybe ... maybe eight?"

"Did they follow us? In one of the other cars?"

"I don't think so."

"But you were focused on me, right?"

Tanner looked stricken. "Car, I didn't—"

"We have to *move*," Carina said, holding on to the pole for support. She looked at the back of the car, where the doors rattled and rocked along with the rhythm of the train.

"If they followed us on, they would already have found us," Tanner said, but he put an arm around Carina's waist and helped her down the aisle. It was slow going—Carina's stomach was twisting and her vision was blurring; she narrowly missed falling on an elderly woman, who glared at them as they passed.

"Or they could be waiting for us at another stop."

"How?"

"It wouldn't have to be them—there could be others. Guards on Sheila's team, watching the platform." The train was beginning to slow as they pulled into the Walnut Creek station. "Come *on*. I'll go through, you stay on this side. They'll be looking for two of us together."

She gave the doors a shove, struggling to open them. Before Tanner could try to stop her, she was in the narrow space between the cars. Below her feet, she could see the tracks rushing by. She closed her hands tighter around the handholds and passed through to the next car. A group of girls in St. Ignatius uniforms sat together near the end of the car; Carina sat behind them and tried to look like she was part of the group, despite her formal dress.

She stared at her lap, hoping it would look like she was

texting, as the train came to a stop. She watched from the corner of her eye as passengers exited and got on: commuters in business clothes, a few older ladies, a young man with a bicycle.

The ride seemed to take forever. At each stop, the train car grew more crowded, giving her extra cover. Every time she saw a young man in a dark jacket, her heart sped up in fear, but no one seemed to pay her any attention. The train went belowground as it traveled under the bay between Oakland and San Francisco; when they arrived at Embarcadero, a dozen passengers exited and someone slid into the seat next to her.

Tanner. "Our stop's coming up," he muttered. He showed her his phone, a map on its display. "Montgomery. That address your uncle gave you? I looked it up. It's in Chinatown, a few blocks from the BART stop. Think you're okay to walk?"

"Yeah, I think so." Carina bit her lip, hoping there wouldn't be anyone waiting for them. "So that dart was meant to knock me out. Sheila wanted them to bring me back."

"And she was willing to go to a lot of trouble to make it happen."

"It's just so crazy," Carina murmured, mindful of all the people within earshot. "I have no idea why she thinks it's so important to get me back there. I mean, I get that she thinks I'm in danger, but it seems like chasing us around with guns is a little extreme."

"Yeah, I was hoping you could maybe shed some light on that," Tanner admitted. "I've got nothing. I can't imagine why anyone would go to so much trouble to save you. I mean, genius hot track stars are pretty much a dime a dozen, you know?"

Carina knew he was trying to lighten the mood, but as the train slowed to a stop, she felt fear grip her again. Fear ... and something else, that strange energy from earlier. She rubbed her arm where the dart had entered and felt nothing, no bump, no swelling. "How are you feeling?" she asked.

"Well, I don't think what I have is a cold. The tremor thing I had earlier, that's gone." Tanner held out his hand with his fingers spread wide: steady. "And even though I feel like I have a fever and I get these weird little waves of—not dizziness ... I guess I'd call it almost like disorientation, my mind trying to catch up to my senses—I don't feel, you know, woozy or anything. I mean, I feel ... strong. Sort of extra sharp or something. Like—" He closed his hand into a fist. "Like I'm not even sure what I could do if I pushed myself. When I went over the cart, when I kicked the box, I was going for distance, and I swear to you, Car, that was the longest jump of my life. It's crazy."

"And the gate," Carina said. "That had to be close to five feet tall."

"Yeah. I mean, I wouldn't have been surprised to see *you* make it, but there's no way I could have cleared that in practice. But when I was coming at it, it was as if my brain did this instant-processing thing where I knew exactly how to land it, and then I had this burst of power to get off the ground."

"Maybe it was the adrenaline?"

They looked at each other, neither expressing aloud what they were both thinking—that there wasn't enough adrenaline in the world to make a feat like that possible.

"What about you?" Tanner asked. "Any other symptoms?"

"I feel feverish too," Carina admitted. "And kind of . . . superfocused? I don't know how to describe it. It's almost like I'm thinking with ten-times magnification."

Tanner laughed. "You are *so* your uncle's niece, you must bleed geek. You have to know that wouldn't make sense to anyone else, right? But yeah, I think I know what you mean."

"Well, maybe it'll at least come in handy. Since we don't exactly know what to expect when we get to Chinatown."

"Nothing like throwing yourself headlong into the unknown," Tanner said. The train was pulling into the Montgomery station, and they stood up to join the knot of passengers heading toward the doors. "Such a rush."

"Tanner . . ." Carina pressed close against him, taking advantage of the crowd to speak into his ear. "I was thinking, maybe you should just turn around. I'll be okay from here, and your parents will be expecting you at home."

Tanner scowled. "First of all, you *won't* be okay from here—at least, I don't have any guarantee that you will, and that's not good enough. There's no way I'm letting you do this by yourself. And second, my parents aren't expecting me until tomorrow."

"What do you mean?"

"I called them, when you were out cold. Told them I was heading over to Rob's."

Rob Stanton was Tanner's best friend at the Borden School, the private school he attended twenty minutes from Martindale. Getting into Borden required both money and an off-the-charts IQ, and Rob was one of the students who came from outside the state for the opportunity and boarded there; Tanner occasionally stayed over in his dorm on weekends.

"I don't like you risking your safety for no good reason," Carina protested. "I mean, it doesn't make any sense for both of us to be here, especially now that there's people *shooting* at us. I would have told you to go home where it's safe."

"I know that. Why do you think I called while you couldn't do anything about it?"

The doors opened and they were swept out with the crowd into the station. Carina put a few feet between her and Tanner, keeping her face down, staying with the crowd moving up the escalator. Moments later they were exiting the station. The evening sky was turning dusky purple. It was cooler in the city, and Carina felt chilly in her light dress. The stolen golf shoes were threatening to give her blisters.

Tanner caught up with her as they crossed Market. "I didn't see anything," he said. "You?"

"No. I think we managed to lose them. And at least here we don't stand out as much." They headed down Sutter Street, blending into the crowd, which represented a wide cross section of humanity. A man in his fifties with silver dreadlocks past his shoulders and a clerical collar stood in a doorway reading a take-out menu. Three young women with neon-colored hair and work boots crossed in front of them at the intersection, and a man in old-fashioned roller skates and a camouflage jacket bought flowers from a vendor across the street.

"Yeah, for all we know, golf shoes are the latest thing here. Or maybe you'll start a trend."

They walked quickly, Carina occasionally looking over her shoulder to see if anyone was following them. They turned right on Stockton into the heart of Chinatown, where paper lanterns festooned the streetlights above the crowded sidewalks. Crowds of people, residents of Chinatown and tourists alike, were out enjoying the beautiful spring evening. Delicious smells wafted from restaurants, and merchants hawked their wares.

"I'm starving," Tanner said as they passed a restaurant whose window tempted passersby with a variety of roasted meats. "I could eat that entire duck myself—as an appetizer."

"Me too. I didn't think I'd be able to eat at all today, but for some reason I'm famished." She'd had to force herself to eat in the days since Walter's death, grief having obliterated her appetite. This morning she'd managed a little breakfast, aware that she had to keep her energy up for the entire day. Still, she hadn't eaten since, and her stomach rumbled ravenously. But they couldn't take a break yet, still terrified that their pursuers were on their trail. "Let's figure out this key thing first and go from there, okay?"

Tanner nodded, glancing at the map on his phone. "We're almost there anyway."

They passed the street twice before realizing it was hidden between two imposing structures: a large restaurant with pagoda-like ornamentation and a multistory brick building with apartments overlooking the street. The "street" was little more than an alley, cobblestones showing through cracked asphalt, laundry hanging high above them, stretching from one building to the other. Tanner took Carina's hand as they threaded their way past people who were using the narrow street as a shortcut between the broad avenues.

Only some of the doors and tiny storefronts along the street were marked. Carina and Tanner nearly missed number 220, the faded, scratched gold numerals almost invisible on a pane of glass in a door that had been propped open. As they hesitated in front of the entrance, a gray blur raced from the dim interior onto the street. Carina bit down a gasp: she was pretty sure it was a rat.

Before she could change her mind, she pulled Tanner into the building. Inside was a tiny foyer lit by a single bulb hanging from the ceiling. Stained, torn red carpeting lined the floor, and peeling patterned wallpaper made the space seem even smaller. To the right was a hallway with four doors; to the left, a staircase.

"Apartment number 2E," Carina said, more bravely than she felt. "Upstairs."

The first step squeaked loudly, and she froze, praying no one would come out of the apartments. The best-case scenario was that they'd be stopped and forced to explain to curious neighbors why they had a key to the apartment; the worst case was much more dangerous: that this was some sort of trap and they were walking right into it.

But Carina couldn't think of any other options.

Tanner stayed right behind her as they climbed. Another naked lightbulb lit the second floor, casting murky shadows down the hall. Three of the doors looked identical—filthy smudges around the brass doorknobs, paint peeling and faded, graffiti scratched here and there.

The fourth door, the one labeled 2E, was a little cleaner than the others, especially in the center, as though someone had started scrubbing it but got tired before working out to the edges. Carina stood in front of it, holding the key in her hand, trying to summon the courage to put it in the lock.

"I don't know . . . ," she whispered.

Tanner pressed his ear against the door, frowning. "Nothing."

He ran his fingers lightly over the surface. "Feel this," he said softly, taking her hand and guiding her fingers across it. There was a faint ridge, invisible in the dim light and almost impossible to detect by touch. Carina slid her fingers along it; the ridge defined a six-inch-square area near the middle of the door, where the paint was slightly smoother.

"What do you think?" Tanner asked.

"I think . . . that there's no way we're going to figure out what's going on if we don't try the key. If it really was Walter who left it for me, he will have left an explanation on the other side of this door."

"And if not?"

Carina shrugged, trying to project a confidence she didn't

feel. "If not, well, we already beat them once, right? Just be ready to *run*."

And with that she put the key in the lock and turned it.

The door didn't open.

She twisted the knob, jimmying the key, but after a second Tanner put his hand on her arm. "Wait," he said quietly. "Look at this."

In the center of the door the edge of the offset square Carina had felt with her fingertips was now visible. As she watched, the almost-invisible gap widened to an eighth of an inch, then a quarter, accompanied by a faint electronic whine. A panel that had been painted to match the door was slowly sliding back, disappearing into the wood. Whatever was underneath the hollowed-out section faintly glowed.

"It's a touch-screen panel," Tanner muttered. As the section that had covered it slid the rest of the way into the door, it revealed a screen that was black except for a single sentence in the center:

The Count of Harewood bids you CHOOSE wisely.

"Oh wow," Carina exclaimed, covering her mouth with her hand. "It really was him. Walter did this."

"*The Count of Harewood?* Who the heck is that?"

"Not *who*, but *what*. It's a classic cryptanalysis problem," Carina said. "A variation on the multi-alphabet Beaufort cipher. Walter taught it to me when I was in grade school. When he came over for Thanksgiving one year, he taught me how to solve it while we waited for the turkey to be ready."

"Huh ... most people would have probably settled for a game of Chutes and Ladders."

"Yeah, well ... not my family. It was the same Thanksgiving my mom put the turkey in the oven while it was still frozen. After four hours there was still ice in the middle. She was totally stressed. We ended up eating Bagel Bites."

Solving the Beaufort cipher that day had been the first time Carina understood how much she loved deciphering puzzles, but she didn't tell Tanner that because a lump was forming in her throat and this was not the time to lose her composure. Her mother had stayed in the kitchen most of that afternoon, on the phone with the Butterball hotline, insisting there had to be *something* they could suggest to fix her ruined meal. She had invited a few interns who worked with her and Walter, and they drank Bloody Marys and polished off an entire cheese tray from the grocery store, watching football on TV and gossiping about people they knew from work. Only Walter had paid any attention to Carina, who had worn her favorite brown corduroy jumper and a turtleneck printed with pumpkins for the occasion.

Even then, she'd longed for a normal family. She wasn't entirely sure what it would look like, but from her friends' lives she gathered that moms cooked for days leading up to the celebration and dads threw footballs around in the backyard with their kids before standing at the head of the table carving the turkey and saying grace.

It wasn't that she wanted any of those things—she

wouldn't know how to play football and she wasn't particularly religious—but her friends, even those who complained about their strict parents and annoying siblings, all seemed to know that they *belonged*. That they were a part of something bigger than just themselves. And Carina hadn't felt that way for as long as she could remember. Yes, she was a daughter, a niece, and she knew that her mother and uncle loved her. But it was as if they were all planets whose orbits never touched, and Carina would have gladly given up some of the autonomy her friends envied to have someone to go home to, to eat her meals with, even to bicker with.

"So, he wants you to translate the word *choose*, I take it?" Tanner said, bringing her back to the moment. "Do you remember how?"

"Of course I do," Carina said. "Now hush."

Tanner was silent while she worked it out in her head. It was complicated, and she had to close her eyes and envision the grid, counting down and across in her imagination to translate each letter, taking into account the one that followed. As she figured out each one, she typed it into the keypad, forcing herself not to rush, hoping the screen wouldn't time out. There was no telling what would happen if she guessed wrong; Walter might have programmed a lockout in the event of missed guesses.

As she typed the last letter, holding her breath, the screen went blank and there was a faint mechanical click as the door opened of its own accord.

"Damn." Tanner whistled softly through his teeth.

"Impressive, right?" Carina couldn't help feeling pleased

with herself, as well as relieved. The door had opened only an inch or two, not far enough to see into the room, but Carina was no longer as leery, knowing that Walter had left the puzzle in the door for her alone. The panel was already closing, sliding back into its camouflage, and Carina slipped the key out of the lock and put it back in her pocket.

"Let me go in first," Tanner said, stepping in front of her.

Carina knew he was trying to protect her, but she was the one who had dragged him into this mess and if something dangerous waited for them, she wasn't about to let him face it alone. She followed close behind as he pushed the door open and entered the room.

It was a small space, illuminated only by the lights from the street that penetrated the thin drapes, neon flashes blinking into the gloom of a tiny studio apartment. It was too dark to make out any details. Carina felt around on the wall for a light switch, and seconds later the room glowed from the light of a single lamp sitting on a battered dresser.

They were alone. A tiny bathroom opened off one wall, but there was no shower curtain, and thankfully no one lurking behind the door. A twin bed frame held a narrow mattress and a neatly folded stack of linens; Carina crouched down and peered underneath just to make sure, but no one hid there. A cheap-looking bookcase held bottled water and packaged nonperishable food.

Tanner shut the door behind them and stood in the middle of the room, hands behind his back, as though worried about disturbing anything.

"Your uncle's home away from home?" he said dubiously. "Doesn't really seem like his style."

Carina laughed. It felt good to let out some of the tension. "Maybe he hadn't gotten around to remodeling yet."

The house she'd shared with Walter had been a grown-up geek bachelor's wonderland: lots of minimalist furniture and expensive electronics, a few houseplants and prints of bridges and skyscrapers. It was obsessively clean and uncluttered. This room was also free of clutter, containing only the bed, dresser, bookcase, and a small desk with a chair, but it was so austere as to be almost jail-like. Whatever Walter had intended the room for, it wasn't comfort.

But he had left his mark in other ways.

The door, for instance. It had closed behind them with barely a sound, gliding shut on some unseen mechanism. Walter had not only fitted the door with the device hidden inside, but also replaced the hinges so it wouldn't slam and draw attention.

The interior of the room also looked unremarkable, but as Carina looked around more carefully, she noticed a few other things.

The windows were barred—from the *inside,* with a grid that looked too lightweight to do the job—until she spotted the wires leading into the wall. A note taped above read DON'T TOUCH.

Carina had to turn away from the familiar handwriting, which made Walter's presence in the room achingly real. Why hadn't he told her about this place? Why hadn't he trusted her with his fears?

There were two items on the desk: a small disposable phone and a black backpack. The phone was brand-new and the backpack was sleek and expensive-looking. Carina put her hand on the backpack, giving it an experimental shove.

"So, you don't think if I open this thing, it'll make the room explode or something?" Carina joked nervously.

"Not if your uncle left it for you. I mean ... seems like he went to a lot of trouble to make sure you were the only person who could get in here. So I'm guessing that's for you."

Carina bit her lip and nodded. Yet again it seemed like she only had one course of action, and it didn't involve caution. She picked up the backpack and carried it to the bed, sitting cross-legged with her back against the headboard. Unzipping the main compartment, she pulled out a laptop, which she set down carefully in front of her. In an outer pocket was an envelope with her name on it in Walter's handwriting, identical to the envelope that had contained the key.

Tanner sat down next to her. "You okay to open that?" he asked softly.

Carina only nodded. She tore open the envelope and upended it on the bed. *Another* key, taped to a piece of paper that was filled with nonsensical text.

And an enormous stack of cash secured with a rubber band.

CHAPTER SIX

Friday, 8:51 p.m.
9:08:51

"How much *is* that?" Tanner asked as Carina flipped through the stack of twenties and hundreds.

"I don't know—a lot. More than we need for anything I can think of."

She handed it to Tanner and picked up the paper. The key was small, the numeral *47* stamped on its orange plastic barrel-shaped head.

"This looks like a locker key. Like the ones used at airports."

Carina stared at the text on the paper. The first line contained only a single word: *AKIYAMA*. Below it was the phrase *Softie's favorite flavor*, followed by a sentence composed of more nonsense words.

"'Softie's favorite flavor,'" Tanner muttered, reading over her shoulder. "Please tell me this isn't a hallucination."

"No, it's just ... Akiyama's a simple columnar transposition with an offset."

"A *what*?"

"It's a kind of code where you take the letters of the message and offset them by a particular interval in the alphabet, and then put them in a specific sequence in a table, where the other table elements are random."

"Oh. Well, that clarifies things, thanks," Tanner said, rolling his eyes. "And *Softie* ... ?"

"Softie was my teddy bear when I was little. Now be quiet so I can concentrate."

She stared at the table of letters while Tanner counted the stack of bills. Something was nagging at her brain, a faint memory involving Uncle Walter and the much-loved, ragged bear she'd dragged around with her until she was six.

Solving an Akiyama code was easy if you knew the key word, but Carina couldn't figure out Walter's hint. She wasn't surprised he'd used Softie, since the bear had been her constant companion for so long and Walter had pretended to talk to it, asking the stuffed animal if he'd had a good day at bear school, if he thought he should wear shoes in the house, if he'd like a snack—

"Barbecue!" Carina exclaimed.

"Uh ..."

"Softie. His favorite flavor was barbecue. Whenever Uncle Walter babysat me, he always had potato chips at his house, and he let me choose what kind, except he pretended to ask Softie and ..."

Her voice trailed off as she found a pen in the little drawer of the desk. "I think I know how to solve this."

"Good. You go ahead and do that. I'm not feeling great. I'm about to die from starvation. You translate and I'll just fan myself with this stack of two thousand dollars and eat one of these." He picked up a small white package from the shelf. "'Datrex Emergency Food Ration Bar. High energy value. Non-thirst-provoking.' Yum."

Carina glanced up. "Did you say two *thousand*?"

"Yeah." Tanner grinned. "Any chance you want to go to Vegas?"

"Uh . . . considering our luck so far today, I think I'll pass."

As Tanner tore the foil off the bar and took a bite, Carina wrote out the grid on the bottom of the piece of paper.

"Hmm," he said, chewing. "This tastes like wood shavings."

Carina ignored him and began translating the characters, one at a time. In moments she had the answer: "It says Civic Center BART. This key must be to a locker in the station."

Tanner looked disappointed. "Seriously? Why not just put whatever he wanted you to have in this room? Since he made sure you were the only person who'd be able to get into it?"

"I don't know. Maybe . . . an extra level of precaution. I mean, it's obvious he thinks this is worth the effort."

"I guess. Listen . . . I was thinking, I'm starving, and here we are in the middle of, like, fifty restaurants in a few square blocks. And whatever's in that locker, it's still going to be there in an hour or two, right? So why don't I go out and get us something to eat. That okay with you?"

Carina hesitated. Now that she'd found the next step in Walter's trail of clues, she wanted to move on to it. But she too was ravenous, and the low-level jitteriness was getting worse, probably because she hadn't eaten. Or maybe it was some lingering effect from whatever was in the dart; her heart seemed to be beating more quickly than usual, and she had the urge to get up and pace or stretch, anything to move her body. Food might settle that feeling as well, and *real* food sounded a lot more appetizing than the square cube that Tanner had eaten.

"I guess we could eat, only maybe I should go. You're better with computers—could you stay here and see what's on the laptop?"

"In my *sleep*." Tanner reached out and gently tucked a stray section of Carina's bangs out of her eyes. "I hate for you to go out there alone, though. We can't be sure that Baxter and whoever didn't take another train, track us here somehow. If they're in Chinatown—"

"You're being paranoid," Carina said with more confidence than she felt. "You saw. No one was interested in us at all out there."

"No one we noticed, true, but, Car, these guys train for this sort of thing, right? They know how to stay out of sight when they need to."

"Okay." She thought for a moment. "I'll get us something, some sort of disguise. There's got to be something in those tourist shops."

"I don't know," Tanner said, drawing her close. "I still don't like it, but I have to admit it makes sense for just one of us to go. But you have to be careful, okay?"

Tanner's touch was both a comfort and a temptation. As Carina leaned against him and closed her eyes, she wished she could just stay here in his arms and pretend that the last few hours hadn't happened. Inhaling his scent and wrapping her arms around him, she thought about how lucky she was to have found him.

A few months of dating had convinced her that what she was feeling was not only first love, but *real* love, the sort that most people rarely experience. The fact that she couldn't bring herself to say so out loud ... well, she was working on that. No one in her family had said "I love you" as far back as she could remember. Carina had tried to say the words to Tanner—three simple syllables, something people everywhere said to each other every day—and yet every time she tried, it was as though her system shut down, interrupting her power of speech and making her heart race. She'd resigned herself to the fact that it would take more time, and Tanner made her feel like he would give her all the time she needed.

She knew that most high school romances ended. But she and Tanner weren't most people, and what they had wasn't what most people had. When Tanner got lost in his coding or she was deep into her computations, it was like they each took a part of the other with them. They could sit next to each other in a crowded café and still be alone ... or they could be alone on a hike in the hills and feel like they had everything they needed, just the air and the sun and each other. Carina's therapist suggested that she clung so hard to Tanner because she'd lost so much, but Tanner was no substitute for a missing dad or dead mother. He wasn't an addiction or a dependency or a crutch. Tanner was just himself, and he fit with her perfectly, as though they were two halves of a whole.

Carina had dated before. Given so much independence by her mother, she'd been free to spend time with boys since middle school, and had never had any trouble attracting their attention. Carina knew it was more about the way she looked than who she was—it wasn't like great math skills were a particularly potent charm—but she didn't care because, until Tanner, she hadn't been looking for anything serious. Someone to hang out with, to impress her friends, to take to school dances.

But Tanner's touch was nothing like the touches of other boys, and he looked at her as if he really *saw* her. Tanner knew what she was thinking even before she said it; sometimes he seemed to know what she was thinking even before *she* knew.

Last night Tanner had called after dinner, asking if she wanted to go out for ice cream. Sheila had agreed reluctantly after Carina convinced her that she needed the distraction, and promised that she would be home well before midnight. Tanner picked her up from Sheila's house in the car he'd borrowed from his dad and announced that there had been a change of plans: they were going to go up on the school's roof to gaze at the stars high in the sky over the valley.

Carina didn't bother to tell Sheila, figuring that since she was new to her role of guardian, she didn't need to sweat the details. When they got to the top of the fire escape ladder and spread out a blanket that faced the long slope down the hill into town, Tanner spent the first few minutes staring at her instead of the stars.

"What," she'd finally said, blushing. "So I got a haircut."

It wasn't just a haircut, of course, but Carina didn't think Tanner would be interested in the detailed list of beauty treatments that ended up on Sheila's bill, which totaled several hundred dollars by the time they were done.

"I like the haircut, but that's not what I'm looking at. You look . . . different, somehow. Sort of . . . lit up."

Carina was about to explain the complicated hair coloring process, the high- and low-lights and gloss treatment, when he'd kissed her. And gone on kissing her. For hours, it felt like, and then the kissing took them further, to the places she'd been wanting to go to for so long. Tanner had stopped several times to ask her if she was sure, until she told him to quit asking. There would never be a better time, a more perfect time, than under the bright moon, the valley dusted with the sparkle of lights below, in the arms of the boy who loved her, who could take away her pain with a smile, a touch, a promise.

Now, as she tried to hold on to the feeling of safety that came from being in his arms, she felt the longing again instead, the heat inside her that Tanner alone could make her feel. But it was overshadowed by fear.

And hunger. Raging, relentless hunger.

She brushed her lips against Tanner's and forced herself

to get up. Taking the bills Tanner had peeled from the stack, she quickly tucked them into her pocket with the key.

"You'll freeze," Tanner said. "It's getting cold out there. Maybe you should buy a sweatshirt."

"I might do better than that, even." Carina pretended she wasn't holding her breath as she slowly turned the doorknob. She trusted Walter; whatever he'd done to this room, she knew it was meant to ensure safety. But still, it was hard not to imagine the place being blown to bits by some hidden trigger, and it was a relief when nothing happened after she pulled open the door.

The hallway was as silent and dark as it had been earlier. Carina eased the door shut behind her; it slid the last few inches by itself, closing with the same solid mechanical click. She tried not to worry about whether the code would work for a second time when she returned with the food.

She had the key; she had the code. Tanner would be waiting for her. It would be enough. It had to.

«◆»

The crowds had thinned. Some of the merchants' doors were shuttered for the evening, but the restaurants were doing brisk business. Carina's stomach went weak with hunger and she found herself salivating.

But first she needed to do one other thing. They couldn't stay hidden in Uncle Walter's secret room forever; they would need to venture out to the BART station at the Civic Center as soon as possible. By now, Sheila would have given their description to more people, all searching for them. It was terrifying to think about, especially since Carina was still having trouble believing that her uncle had been working on something so sensitive that armed men were hunting her down for it. But the worst-case scenario was that a small army of trained agents knew that she and Tanner had boarded the inbound BART train and were looking for them in the city. If they had somehow figured out that Carina and Tanner had exited at the Montgomery stop, it greatly increased the chances that they were nearby.

So Carina had to make sure that she and Tanner were invisible.

Two blocks from the apartment, Carina found a brightly lit souvenir shop on Stockton. Racks of postcards and novelty key chains gave way to T-shirts and caps and inexpensive sportswear inside the crowded store. She shopped quickly, guessing at Tanner's sizes. When she was finished, she had filled a big plastic shopping bag with purchases; the bored clerk barely glanced at Carina as he rang her up.

Carina's next stop was at a busy restaurant. The woman working the register merely grunted and pointed when Carina asked for a take-out menu. Carina didn't recognize most of the dishes, which were described in Chinese and broken English, so she just pointed at items in each section. Finding a chair tucked between the kitchen door and a large plant, she sat down and waited. She kept her eye on the entrance, watching as pedestrians strolled by the tall windows.

When she saw a man in a black track jacket with his hand at his ear, she shrank back against the wall.

Was that the lab logo, stitched onto his jacket? She thought she saw a flash of red and silver, but maybe it was just the bright neon lights reflecting off the glass. It was possible that he'd just been running his hand through his close-cropped hair, not adjusting an earpiece—and that Carina was becoming way too paranoid.

She thought about Baxter. He had the training and resources that could keep them safe. She was certain, if she called him, he'd do whatever he could to help. Maybe he could get them out of the area, to another city where Sheila would never think of searching.

But if Sheila found out, there would be hell to pay. If she knew he'd betrayed her, then he would be in danger too. Maybe there was a way he could do something behind the scenes, perhaps direct the search away from Carina and Tanner.

The taciturn woman placed two large white plastic bags on the counter, interrupting Carina's spinning thoughts. Carina paid quickly and asked if there was a back entrance to the restaurant. If the woman found the request odd, she didn't let on; she motioned down the hall and muttered something Carina didn't understand.

Threading her way through the crowded restaurant, she kept her head down, continuing past the restrooms and down a dank hall to a small door propped open into an alley. The smell of garbage and car exhaust assaulted her. Behind the buildings, workers emptied trash into the Dumpsters and carried boxes from loading docks. Carina was getting the feeling that Chinatown never slept, and she was glad for the commotion as she hurried down the street in the direction of the apartment.

She missed her turn the first time but eventually found her way back to the tiny street, breathing a sigh of relief when she was finally back inside the dim lobby. When she got to the apartment, the door opened by itself, startling her so much that she almost dropped her shopping bags. Tanner reached through the narrow opening and pulled her in.

"How did you know I was back?" she asked as soon as she was safely inside.

"Because your uncle's a genius. Look at this."

He showed her a small square mirror mounted on the wall of the bathroom. Carina bent her face closer, as Tanner instructed, and found that she was somehow looking out into the hallway.

"It's all mechanical," Tanner explained. "It's not a camera; he did it with mirrors. I checked it out. There are tons of tiny mirrors mounted at angles. There are holes in the ceiling, so he had to have figured out how to get into the space above the ceiling. It's a completely low-tech way to see what's in the hall."

"He probably just did it to amuse himself," Carina said, feeling a pang of sadness. Walter had been a tinkerer; he'd rebuilt old shortwave radios for fun. On the surface, it was a contradiction—a technology master devising alternate solutions to problems that could be easily solved with technology—but it just underscored her uncle's curiosity and love of discovery.

"Whatever." Tanner shrugged. "I still think it's genius."

"Yeah." Carina wiped her eyes. "Uh, can we eat? I agree Walter's the greatest, but I'm starving."

"I have more to show you, but if I don't eat something soon I'm going to pass out."

It ended up taking less than half an hour to get through dinner. The dishes included soup and some sort of dumpling and pork and tofu dishes, enough to feed four hungry people, but Carina couldn't stop eating until every bit was gone. Tanner too seemed ravenous.

"Wow," he said with wonder when there was nothing left but the white cardboard containers and a few packets of soy sauce. "I wonder if that was some sort of delayed stress reaction."

"In both of us?" Carina said dubiously, putting the trash back in the bags and tying them shut. "Unlikely. What did you find while I was gone, anyway?"

Tanner tapped the laptop's touch pad and the screen sprang to life, showing a list of files, most of them with numeric names.

"I opened a few of the most recent," Tanner said apologetically. "They're video files. I didn't want to watch without you, when I saw what they were. Carina . . . your uncle recorded himself talking, here in this room."

" 'Play me first, Carina,' " she read, squinting at the file list. "Seriously? That's what the file's called?"

"I guess he didn't want to leave anything up to chance."

"This was recorded three days before he died. Does that mean he was here then?"

"Well, yeah, unless he hacked the internal clock or FTP'd the file onto the laptop."

"Uh ... in English?"

"Well, let's just say he would have had to go to a lot of trouble. Besides, Carina, why would he modify the date on a file he wanted you to have?"

The knot that Carina had been carrying in her gut all day, grief wrapped in layers of fear and adrenaline, pressed on her lungs and deprived her of breath. Uncle Walter had left her a message in the form of a file. How long had he suspected that he was going to be killed?

"Play it," she said, before she could change her mind.

Tanner leaned against the headboard next to her and propped the computer on his knees. Wordlessly, he clicked on the file.

There was Uncle Walter, wearing his favorite sweater, a heather-blue one made for hiking even though the closest he ever came to hiking was pacing the halls of the house when he was trying to solve some problem. She tried to remember if he had worn it that morning—it had been unexpectedly chilly that week, so he very well could have chosen this sweater.

"Hey, Carrie," he said into the camera with a wobbly smile. Tears popped into Carina's eyes: he was the only person in the world who was allowed to call her Carrie.

He cleared his throat. "Uh, this is kind of weird because if you're seeing this, well ..." He stared down at his lap. "I mean, it's not good, right? But what's important now, no matter what else has happened, is that you do exactly what I say. If you got this far, then you got my message to avoid Sheila. I'm so sorry about that. She fooled me, Carrie. She fooled us all."

Tanner squeezed Carina's hand. "You okay watching this?"

She nodded, not wanting to miss a word.

"I can't even begin to tell you how sorry I am to put you in this position. I never wanted . . . I can't stand the thought of anything happening to you. So what I need you to do is to take care of yourself. Keep yourself safe, Carrie, I mean it. There are other files on this computer that will expose secrets that will get a lot of people in trouble. You need to get in touch with Major Nathan Wynnside with the Army Criminal Investigation Command. I've told him about my, uh . . . situation. He is expecting to hear from me when I return from Houston. If anything happens to me, I have told him that someone else will be in touch. This is the phone number you should call." He slowly and clearly recited a string of numbers. "Do not call from this room. Take the phone that I have left for you on the desk and go somewhere safe. A public location is best, a busy park or a shopping center. Call using that phone—not your own phone, Carrie, that is very important—and tell Major Wynnside where to look. I know you'll be able to figure that out from my note. Don't worry about it being locked. For the major, this will not be a problem. The key is only a spare."

He paused and drew a breath, appearing to consider what to say next. "You should never need to go to that place yourself, Carrie. What is contained in that locker . . . I do not want you connected with it in any way. The other files on this computer describe what we have been working on, the project that has consumed us for the last few years. If you watch them, I think you'll understand. Our work, the things we have created, they must never be allowed to fall into the wrong hands. And, Carrie, if you have access to them, then you automatically become a target. I—"

Walter's voice broke, and he cleared his throat before continuing. "I couldn't bear it if anything happened to you. Too much has been lost already. Anyway, after you call Major Wynnside, you must make sure you are safe, so return to this room and *stay here*. There's enough food and water to last you many days. Watch the news and you'll know when it's safe to return home. I have a feeling things will move quickly once Major Wynnside is involved, but I don't think we can be too careful in this case."

Walter paused, looking deeply into the camera. "Well, that's it, then, I guess. Like I said at the beginning . . . Carrie, if you are watching this, then the worst has happened, and I won't get another chance to say this. So I want you to know that you have been the greatest joy in my life. I love you."

He gave a last, weak smile and the clip ended.

CHAPTER SEVEN

Friday, 10:27 p.m.
7:32:20

Tears spilled down Carina's cheeks. Her uncle had been buried today, and she would never get to hug him again, never get to tell him how much she loved him in return. He'd never said it out loud when he was alive. She hadn't doubted his love, but they weren't the kind of family who said it with words.

She wished they had been.

Tanner hadn't let go of her the whole time, holding her close against him. He gently brushed the tears from her face. "You okay?"

"Yes, I think so," Carina said. It was so tempting to sink into the comfort Tanner offered, to stay here where it seemed safe, but they had bigger problems now. "Let's just figure out what to do next."

"Well, according to the video, Walter left you an untraceable disposable phone. You walk out there onto the streets like any other tourist and call this Major Wynnside and give him the locker number at the BART station, and he takes it from there."

"It would have to lead to Sheila getting arrested," Carina mused. "I mean, whatever Uncle Walter left for the major must be enough to incriminate her and whoever she's working with."

"And then you'd be clear too."

"Yeah, and I could go . . . home." Carina hated the way her voice hitched on the last word. She didn't have a home to go to. There was the house she'd shared with Walter, but did she still have a right to live there now? Walter had provided for her financially, but had he also left her a place to live? She'd inherited some money from her mother too, but Walter had taken care of all the details. Carina had no idea where to start to track it all down.

"You know you can stay with us," Tanner said. "My folks would love to have you. It's only a month until graduation, and—"

"Thanks," Carina said quickly, cutting him off. "Seriously. We can figure all that out as soon as we get through this."

Staying with the Sloans sounded good. Better than good—they were a real family, the kind Carina had never had, with a mom and dad and annoying little brothers. They had a big, comfortable house with a white picket fence and a rose garden and an American flag flying over the front door. There was family movie night and football in the backyard and a chore chart. The worst thing that ever happened at the Sloans' was arguing over whose turn it was to do the dishes, or enduring an embarrassing family nickname.

But now Carina had dragged Tanner into a world of trouble. She couldn't imagine involving his family too, not until the danger was past and there was no chance of it resurfacing.

"Tanner." She swallowed, overwhelmed by what she had to say. "Sheila knows who you are. If she thinks she could use you to get to me . . . I'm worried about your family."

"That's ridiculous, Car, I don't have any connection to the lab. She's got to know I don't have anything they can use."

"No, but . . . she knows I care about you. She might try to use you to get me to give her the information. Can't you maybe just call your mom and tell them to be careful?" She looked down at her hands. "Or just go. Tanner, you should just go home. If you're there, Sheila can be sure you aren't helping me, and then—"

But Tanner's face had gone white. He dug for his phone and stared at it in horror. "Oh shit," he said. "You just made me realize something, I've got to . . ."

He leapt off the bed and looked frantically around the room. He settled on a can of generic peas and grabbed it off the shelf. Laying the phone on the desk, he began hitting it over and over with the can, smashing it to pieces. He sorted through the shards, picking up a tiny square chip between his finger and thumb, and whacked it hard.

"Tanner, stop it. Someone's going to hear you!"

"Two things," he said grimly, placing the smashed electronic bit almost gently on the table next to the destroyed phone. "First, I bet your uncle has soundproofed this place. Wouldn't surprise me if there's all kinds of insulation under the floors and behind the walls. And second, every cell phone in America has a tracking device built in. I don't think they could hack it this fast, but with the right access and equipment, they could identify exactly where we are."

Carina stared at the shards of plastic and metal and silicon. "But not anymore, I take it."

"Yeah. And there's no way they could have been on it already," he said, sounding slightly less certain. "Not in that amount of time. I mean, tracing it would be pretty straightforward, but getting the number would be hard, even for them."

"And mine's back in that alley." Carina couldn't remember the exact moment she'd dropped her purse; it hadn't made it on the BART train with her.

"I'll bet it was untraceable anyway. There's a reason your uncle wouldn't let you have a smartphone, and it wasn't because he didn't trust you." Tanner frowned, took a deep breath and rubbed his eyes.

"Hey, are you all right?"

"Yeah, I am. . . . I just feel off, like my senses aren't reacting properly. Like I'm forgetting to blink or something."

Carina knew the feeling, which was strange, because it was difficult to put into words. Whatever Tanner was coming down with, she had it too. "Kind of like there's too much stimulation, right? Like the colors are too bright and the sounds too loud?"

"Yeah, and like I have too much energy. I mean, I feel like

I just need to *move*." He shrugged sheepishly, as though the admission embarrassed him. But Carina had noticed something else—something she didn't want to mention because she didn't know what it meant, and it scared her: his eye had begun to twitch more frequently at the corner. Just like hers. "Look, forget it, I'm sure I'm fine. Listen, you want to check out a couple more of the videos? Might help us figure out what Walter was really doing."

He picked up the laptop and tapped the keyboard as they looked at the file list together.

"Try Project Venice Overview," Carina said, watching him carefully; the twitch subsided.

The file opened and as the video prepared to play, she saw that it was Uncle Walter, in this same room. He was wearing different clothes, and the room was rearranged slightly: he was sitting in the desk chair off to the side. She could see the door to the bathroom in the corner of the screen. He must have set the recording device on the desk to take the video.

"My name is Walter Xavier Monroe," he said in a clear, somber voice. "I am employed as a senior lead analyst at Calaveras National Laboratory." He went on to give his employee ID and Social Security numbers.

"I have been working on Project Venice, which was undertaken by the Calaveras laboratory in March of 2010 after meetings with several branches of the armed services. I was not a part of those initial meetings, and my role has been strictly developmental. Our intent has been to create a synthetic virus to improve performance of US forces on the battlefield."

"Wait," Carina said. Tanner paused the video. "*Virus?* I—I've never heard of anything like this. Not from Walter or my mom."

"I don't know what to tell you," Tanner said. "You want to keep watching?"

She nodded, and Tanner hit play. As Walter talked, she realized with growing horror that she'd known nothing about his work. And that it was a project that had gone very wrong.

The virus had been under development for years. Walter and Sheila and the rest of the team, including her mother, had been trying to isolate a virus that could enhance a soldier's abilities for a short period of time in battle. The current version had what Uncle Walter called, with bitter irony, "the biggest potential." It sharpened all five senses, making them more acute; it caused spikes in the production and release of adrenaline and other hormones and neurotransmitters, resulting in short-term improvement in strength, mental processing speed and acuity, and sensory perception and processing. Reaction times were markedly improved, and both fine and gross motor skills showed dramatic increases. The virus could be delivered directly into the bloodstream and had an extremely low rejection rate, and the microbes reproduced at a rate of one million percent within half an hour of delivery. It was not airborne and could be transmitted from one human to another only via saliva or blood contact, which was most effectively done in the first few hours after infection.

"A breakthrough like this could dramatically reduce casualty rates among US forces," Walter said. "Incidents of fatigue, failure to advance position, friendly fire—we used various modeling to show that all of these could be curbed significantly. There was so much excitement during the first year of the study. It was classified top-secret, but we were assured that the project had the enthusiastic support of the government agencies involved, and there was a feeling of optimism among all of us.

"That was the good news," Uncle Walter said, his voice tired. "Unfortunately, it was followed by a lot of bad news. For one thing, most iterations of the virus were plagued by a range of unpleasant symptoms. For most people, these were mild and included fever, increased appetite, dizziness, fainting, and mild arrhythmia, but for slightly less than two percent of the population there was a risk of heart failure. Slightly more than three-quarters of the test subjects experienced uncontrollable movements, mostly facial tics in the early stage and, later, gross-motor interruptions and even seizures."

"Wait," Carina said. "That's, I mean—"

She didn't finish her sentence, not wanting to miss anything Walter was saying, but those were *their* symptoms, the things she and Tanner had been feeling since this morning. The racing heart, the appetite, the enhancements to their senses and strength—even the twitching.

"... begins to mutate and degrade after twelve hours. The virus begins to attack brain and spinal tissue, causing interrupted neural response, seizures, and motor failure. In the early studies using laboratory subjects, these symptoms were apparent between eight and twelve hours after infection. At thirty-six hours, the virus could not be reversed, even if the antidote was administered. Death followed within thirty-six to thirty-nine hours of infection in every case."

Tanner gripped her hand. Wordlessly, they exchanged a glance.

"Results have been remarkably consistent across test populations." Walter looked directly into the camera, his jaw set, his eyes haunted. "A decision was made at the highest levels to begin human testing. Neither I nor any member of my team was consulted in this matter. Testing did not take place on-site. I cannot speculate as to where it took place or who participated. Nor do I wish to say how I came to be apprised of the results. Following an unauthorized test—unauthorized by me, that is to say—in which a subject died, I demanded that the project be suspended pending investigation. I was assured that this investigation was under way and that the parties responsible for the . . . errors had been removed from participation in the project."

Walter paused and took a deep, shuddering breath. He rubbed his hand across his face but could not erase his haunted expression.

"Oh my God," Carina whispered. "Tanner, those symptoms—they're ours. Everything he described. We have the virus. Somehow Sheila gave it to us."

"You don't know that," Tanner objected, but his face was white. "We've been under a lot of stress, it's been a hell of a day—"

"That doesn't explain it," Carina interrupted. "It doesn't explain *this*."

She pointed to her eye. The skin around it spasmed, causing her to blink rapidly.

She had no idea how they had been infected, but it made a horrible kind of sense. The virus being developed at Calaveras Lab—the one she was supposed to have important knowledge about, information that could get her killed—the one that Sheila said had gotten Uncle Walter murdered. Had it been in the dart that had knocked her out? But what about Tanner—why was he affected? And they'd had the symptoms well before she had been shot. Was this her death sentence?

"You have it too," she whispered, touching Tanner's face.

He covered her hand with his, swallowing hard. "If that's true . . . if it turns out you're right—I just don't understand how it could have happened."

"Let's watch to the end. Hit play."

On-screen, Walter cleared his throat and took another deep breath. "We've been working on a virucide based on research initially conducted by Madelyn Jane Monroe, who died in June of last year. We developed a version of the antidote that completely eradicated the virus from the system, but was very complicated and expensive to produce.

"I and several colleagues were encouraged by the development of the antidote, and were working on attaching it to the virus-delivery mechanism in a time-release formulation. The idea was that when a subject was infected, he would also receive the antidote and we would control the period of time in which the infection would be active. But early testing among animal populations failed almost universally. The attachment mechanism is extremely complicated. Meanwhile, there was mounting pressure among our military sponsors to proceed with what was, in my mind, an unacceptable pairing of the infection with external delivery of antidote. A schism developed within our group, between those who favored pushing forward with testing in the human population and those of us who wanted further restrictions in place. I became, ah, quite vocal in my objections, and on March eleventh of this year I was dismissed from the team and assured that all of my concerns were being evaluated and addressed. I was told that I was needed on another project." Walter laughed bitterly. "But seeing as there were already several of my colleagues, all of them far more qualified than I, heading up the new area I was assigned to, it was hard to view this as anything but an attempt to shut me up. I was sanctioned and forbidden to discuss my work. Most worrisome of all to me was that a new leader was assigned to serve in an exclusive liaison capacity, meaning that project reporting went directly, and only, through her."

Carina felt her gut tighten, certain of what she would hear next. "That employee is Sheila Boylston. It pains me to say that I feel certain Sheila did not discontinue the field studies, but has actually widened their scope. I have further learned that she is receiving funding from outside sources. These include foreign interests. I have reason to believe that discussions are under way to sell the virus to foreign governments for their use in domestic and international battle. Needless to say, there would be no system in place for ensuring the antidote was made available whenever the virus is administered. Soldiers and innocent citizens would be put at unacceptable risk. My belief is that Sheila is taking bids for the technology and means to profit personally, along with hand-selected members of her team, from the sale of Project Venice data. While this violates lab policy as well as federal law, I am most concerned that the virus could be deployed in uncontrolled environments before year's end, without the benefit of incorporated antidote. The risks, I cannot stress enough, are enormous.

"I made a decision to continue working on the antidote on my own. After the death of Madelyn Monroe, I gained access to her private work and refined the antidote. I have developed a version that attaches well to the virus. When injected, the virus is effectively canceled out after twenty-four hours in the body. At this time, I have given no one else access to the improved antidote, and I have grave reservations about ever putting it into production. There are too many variables in the battle arena to ensure that soldiers . . ."

Walter's voice trailed off, his eyes moving to a point off-screen. "I have detailed my concerns elsewhere. I have also been in touch with Major Nathan Wynnside and am preparing a detailed analysis of Project Venice to date, along with a proposal for the destruction of all data and stores of the virus.

"Project Venice has strayed from our initial charge, which was to assist the men and women of our armed services. We never set out to develop supercharged battle drones, at the same time risking lives and turning people into expendable weapons. I implore you to consider the implications of allowing this research to continue. I believe you will reach the conclusion I have, which is that the only ethical resolution is complete termination of the project and destruction of all research conducted to date."

Walter stopped speaking and fumbled with something out of view, ending the video. For a moment neither Carina nor Tanner said anything.

"We have it," Carina whispered. "Whatever it is they made, we have it. We're infected. And we have so little time before—" Her voice broke. "Before it's too late."

"He's figured out how to make the antidote, Carina. Maybe the version we got—maybe it's that kind. It'll destroy itself and we'll be all right."

Carina could see that Tanner didn't believe it any more than she did, that he was saying it just for her. "I just don't understand why. Unless . . ."

Unless this was the ultimate threat, the one thing Sheila could hold over their heads to make them do exactly what she wanted: without her, they couldn't get the antidote.

Without her, they would die.

CHAPTER EIGHT

Friday, 11:32 p.m.
06:26:48

"Even if we go to Sheila, I don't have anything to give her," Carina said. "Walter didn't tell me anything."

Tanner pointed to the locker key. "You have whatever is in the locker. What he wanted Major Wynnside to have. All you have to do is tell her that if she gives us the antidote, you'll tell her where the locker is."

"Maybe Walter left the antidote in the locker."

"Seems unlikely. He wouldn't have had any reason to think you would ever need it."

"Yeah, I guess so. But if we tell Sheila we'll trade with her, what guarantee do we have that she'll keep her promise?" Carina said. "Once she has the key, there's no reason for her to help us."

"Do we have a choice?" Tanner's voice was quiet.

"If we have the virus, we only have thirty-six hours from the time it happened. And I have a pretty good idea when I was infected. It had to be at the salon."

Carina had been wrapped in a plush bathrobe, reclining in a big chair while an aesthetician gave her a facial, and then—a second woman had entered the room. She was dressed in the salon's uniform, a pink blouse embroidered with its signature black lotus leaves, and she'd had a murmured conversation with the first woman, who soon left the room. This new woman announced that she would be taking care of hair removal. "When they waxed my brows, it hurt like hell. There was this stinging ... it would have been so easy. My eyes were closed the whole time, and they could have injected me then and I'd never have known. I mean, it sounds crazy—"

"It sounds *likely*," Tanner said. "Remember who sent you to the salon. Who picked up the bill. Who could have easily bribed someone to let her own person come into the room, or even to do the injection herself. There's a dozen different ways she could have done it, but the bottom line, Car, is Sheila infected you."

"But what about you?"

"I think that part was an accident." Tanner blushed. "You came home from the salon, and I picked you up a little after nine. We were up on the roof by nine-thirty, and then—I mean, Walter said that the virus could be passed through saliva. . . ."

Carina remembered the way Tanner had kissed her with increasing passion, the moment when she knew it wouldn't be enough, that nothing less than everything would be enough.

"Oh my God," she whispered. "*I* did this to you. It's my fault you're infected."

"No," Tanner said grimly. "You can't think like that. It's *her* fault. Sheila, and whoever she's got helping her."

"So if we're right, I've been infected for . . ." Carina glanced at the time on the laptop: it was already after eleven-thirty. "They did my brows at six. I remember because the salon was supposed to close at six and they made a big deal about staying open a few minutes late to finish with me. I mean, no wonder, if Sheila paid them off! So that's—yes . . . almost thirty hours ago. Which means I've only got six left. And you've got a few more."

"Three more. Nine hours." Tanner grimaced, then forced a neutral expression. "So the virus is already breaking us down, which explains the tremors." He held out his hand, which had begun shaking again. Almost at the same moment, Carina felt a vein in her neck spasm. The tics were minor—so far—but the idea of them worsening was terrifying.

"Tanner, let me see that." She reached for the laptop, scrolling to the top of the file list. She found the one she'd noticed before, *Subject Two: Hours 24–38,* and clicked on it. As the file loaded, she didn't meet Tanner's eyes; she wasn't sure she was really ready to find out how she was going to die.

On the screen, a young man in a plain gray T-shirt and khaki fatigue pants stood at the edge of a field. It was an overcast day, a slate sky reaching down to the mountains far in the distance. The man looked like a soldier, with his hair cut short, his arms and chest muscular under the tight shirt. Then again, he could have been a member of the lab's security force. His expression was neutral, until his shoulder jerked—twice, in quick succession. A look of confusion passed over his features.

In the corner of the screen, a digital time stamp ticked the seconds. It read 21:18:02. There was the sound of a man clearing his throat, and then an off-camera voice said, "Field test two, twenty-one hours eighteen minutes after initial infection."

At the crack of what Carina recognized as a starter pistol, the kind used in state track competitions, the man took off running. The camera followed, in the jerky, wobbling fashion that indicated someone was filming while running along beside him, and an obstacle course covering several acres of the field came into view. The man scaled a rope wall, leaping nimbly from the top to the ground on the other side, and instantly began running again. He worked his way through a series of structures built out of raw timber and lumber; some required him to climb, others to crawl or to hang and move hand-over-hand. Everything he did, he seemed to do at a heightened speed; tasks that would be nearly impossible for most people looked effortless. When he finished the course, he jogged back to his original position at the edge of the field. The off-camera voice recited his time and added a single word: "Phenomenal."

The scene changed to a small room with white walls, gray carpet, and no windows. The time stamp in the corner of the screen read 35:14:08. The same young man, his hair wet from a shower, was sitting on an industrial-looking cot, dressed in a white T-shirt and gray sweatpants. The room looked a lot like a jail cell except for the carpet and the presence of a closed door instead of bars. From the angle, it was clear that the camera was mounted to the ceiling. "How are you feeling?" the offscreen voice asked—the same voice as before, but this time tinny and mechanical, as if it was coming from a speaker.

"All right." The man looked alert, his eyes wide and bright, but there was an anxious quality to his fleeting smile. Sweat beaded his brow. It looked like it took effort to appear unruffled. His hands were clenched in his lap and he blinked every few seconds. One foot appeared to move uncontrollably, shuffling in place.

Carina gasped: it was only forty-five minutes before the thirty-six hour mark. If the man didn't receive the antidote soon, he would die.

"All of your test results came back—truly an excellent effort," the voice said.

"Thank you." The man seemed to wince as his leg jerked twice. He grabbed his shin with his hands, as if to keep it anchored.

"We discussed the lack of sleep. You won't be able to, so you might as well not try. You've had slightly under seven thousand calories today, but you may still feel hungry. This is normal. Try to stay calm."

"Yes, sir."

Then the video sped up. It took a moment for Carina to

realize what was happening because the man kept sitting on the cot, then he got up and began to pace. His movements were rapid and jerky, showing that the tape speed had been increased. He seemed to grow increasingly agitated, pacing the room and, it looked like, talking to himself. Eventually screaming, though after the tape increased in speed there was no sound.

The speed slowed to normal again, the time 36:30:11. "He's going to die," Carina whispered, holding Tanner's hand tightly.

"Do you want me to shut it off?" Tanner's voice was hoarse.

"No. I have to see." The man stumbled around the room, taking off one shoe and then the other, pelting the walls with them. One crashed near the camera, and the image flickered. The blinking had developed into a full-fledged spasm, one entire side of his face twitching and twisting as he began bumping into the walls as though he couldn't see them.

The tape jumped ahead, the time stamp changing to 36:50, 37:18, 38:22. The action slowed whenever the man did something new. He tore off his shirt as though contact with the fabric was hurting him; he tugged at his belt buckle for a while but eventually gave up, his fingers trembling too violently for the task. The discarded shirt lay in the middle of the room and he stepped on it as if it weren't there. He never sat down, never rested. By hour 38 he was screaming nonstop, the muscles in his neck bulging.

Then he started hitting the wall. Tanner's hand tightened

on Carina's as the man slammed his fist, over and over. When blood appeared, Tanner reached to turn off the recording.

"No," Carina whispered, her throat dry. She pushed his hand away. "I have to see."

The man no longer resembled the one who'd performed so well earlier. His face was a rictus of agony and fury. He kicked and punched the walls until they were soiled with his blood. One of his wrists hung at an odd angle, as if he'd broken his own bones with the force of his blows.

Then he turned on himself.

He'd managed to pull the hair out of his bleeding scalp and gashed his face with his own fingernails when Carina couldn't take any more, and closed the file. The time read 38:39:44.

Carina forced herself to take deep breaths. "The virus attacks the brain and then it makes you attack yourself."

Tanner's face was white. "We are not going to let that happen to us."

"I infected you," Carina said miserably. "If it wasn't for me, you'd be fine."

"Stop it, Car. Don't think like that. Last night was ... I wouldn't trade it for anything. We just have to find the antidote."

"In less than six hours?"

"Well, look on the bright side—we won't need any sleep. We might have to eat again in an hour. . . ." Tanner smiled weakly.

Carina felt hysteria tug at her, the horror of the situation and her guilt for dragging Tanner into it making her want to scream. But she had to stay rational if they were to have any hope of survival.

A buzzing from the desk made her jump—the disposable phone that Walter had left her. Carina stared at it as though it were a snake getting ready to strike.

"Should I answer?"

"I think you have to, just so we know what we're dealing with."

Carina picked it up as though it were a ticking bomb. "Hello?"

"Carina? Carina Monroe?"

The voice was mechanical, raspy and monotone. Carina couldn't tell if it was a man or a woman; a device of some sort was definitely being used to modify it. "Who is this?"

"I'm looking for Carina Monroe. I am a ... friend of your uncle Walter. I am in a position to help you. Right now you're in a lot of danger. I just need to know where you are and I can pick you up and take you somewhere where I can guarantee your safety."

Carina frantically reviewed the list of people who might have an interest in helping her *and* the means to do it. There was no one, except maybe Baxter, and he wouldn't need to disguise his voice.

Lots of people had taken an interest in Carina—her teachers, her track coaches, her college admissions counselors. A few neighbors. Tanner's parents—they'd been wonderful to her. The parents of a few other friends. But how would any of them—how would anyone at all—have this cell number?

Besides, none of those people had any idea that Walter had been involved with something dangerous. Carina herself hadn't known until this afternoon.

Twenty-four hours ago she had trusted Sheila completely. She probably would have trusted this stranger on the phone, assuming that Walter had set up a safety net for her. But in the end, Walter hadn't even been able to protect himself.

"Are you still there?" the voice asked. Carina gently pressed the end button on the phone.

"Not anymore," she said softly.

CHAPTER NINE

Friday, 11:56 p.m.
06:03:09

"Nothing," Tanner said. It had only taken him a couple minutes to change into the clothes Carina had bought him, and then he'd taken the phone apart, looking for tracking devices or anything suspicious. As he reassembled it, using the specialized multi-tool set he used as a key chain, Carina made last-minute preparations in front of the bathroom mirror.

Disguising Tanner had been easy: Carina had bought him a T-shirt with a graphic design of the Golden Gate Bridge. A pair of shorts—they were a little too baggy, but at least they stayed up. And Converse sneakers, since that was all the shop carried—black ones customized with orange stitching and the Giants logo. He looked like any other tourist in town to see the sights and maybe catch a game—

all he needed was a sunburn and he'd be indistinguishable from the crowd that gathered at Pier 39.

Carina was having a little more trouble. The black running shorts and tank top she'd chosen to give her freedom of movement were fine. But the hat that had seemed like such a good idea in the store—a baseball cap with a fake platinum-blond ponytail attached in the back—wasn't working. She couldn't get her own long hair to stay tucked up in the cap.

"Can I borrow that?"

"This?" He handed her the multi-tool. When she opened the scissor attachment, he said, "Oh," and she had to turn away.

He'd once told her that her hair was the first thing he noticed the day they met at the climbing gym. It was early autumn last year, and they both used the same gym between seasons. Climbing was an excellent total-body workout for Carina, but for Tanner, it was also a way to keep his arms in shape for the javelin, shot put, and discus.

He told her he'd known, that first day, that he could pass her on the climbing wall. It wasn't bragging—to throw a twelve-pound shot almost twenty meters, you had to have developed both a certain level of strength and finely tuned agility. But when Tanner looked up and saw Carina's long, silky ponytail gleaming in the gym's skylights, bouncing against her bare shoulder blades, he decided to hang back and let her believe she'd beat him instead.

Carina had climbed with determination, oblivious to the fact that she was being watched. She took a difficult route, pushing herself to develop her reach. At the point when she overshot and was about to fall, Tanner said he caught his breath as she clung, suspended, trying to regain her footing on a plastic hold that was just out of reach, the whole time her hair shimmering and bobbing in the sunlight.

The first time Tanner kissed her he'd wound his hands through her hair, the strands slipping through his fingers. Even when they were just watching TV, he liked to play with it, rubbing the ends almost as though he wasn't aware he was doing it.

Carina blinked away the memories and clenched her jaw as she made the first cut. It felt like she was cutting some connection between them.

Tanner put his hand over hers, stopping her. "Let me," he said gently. He worked quickly, both of them aware of the critical seconds ticking away, but in moments he'd given her a shoulder-length cut that was surprisingly even, considering the tools he had to work with.

Carina shook out the loose hairs, peering at her reflection. She didn't hate the look the way she'd expected. She looked like herself but also . . . like someone else.

Carina had never known her father. She became an orphan when her mother died, and when Walter died, she was truly on her own. The girl looking back at her, with her light-brown hair curving toward her chin with a wave that Carina didn't know she had, looked . . . strong. Capable. Confident.

"Thank you," she said, knowing there wasn't time now to explain it to Tanner. "You can add that to your resume.

Hairdresser. Bet there will be high demand for that next year in the dorms at Berkeley."

There was one more thing she had to do before they left. She picked up the disposable phone and dialed from memory.

Sheila answered on the first ring. "Hello?"

"It's me," Carina said.

"Oh my God, Carina, I've been worried sick about you!" Sheila said. She was pretty convincing, actually, managing to inject a note of hysteria into her voice. Except there had been a tiny hesitation, a beat of silence before she spoke, and Carina knew she'd been figuring out her next move.

Sheila was cagey. But Carina was only now learning exactly how clever she could be. And she wasn't falling for it again.

"You infected me. I want the antidote. Enough for me and Tanner."

"What? You think *I* infected you? I would *never* intentionally put you at risk."

"Oh, come on, Sheila, *please*. The research you and Uncle Walter were doing? The virus that turns soldiers into killing machines? We saw the video. You know, the one where the guy tears his face off at the end?"

Carina heard Sheila suck in her breath sharply. "What— you—how did you—"

"Turns out Walter left us a few clues, or we wouldn't have any idea what's in store for us. Very clever, with the whole brow-wax thing."

"Carina, I don't know what you think you've seen, but I

promise you, all I want is to keep you safe. If you just let me come pick you up, we can sort through all of—"

"I just want the antidote. You say you're concerned about my safety, prove it. We can pick a nice public location and you can give me the antidote. When Tanner and I are sure we're back to normal, *then* we can have this conversation."

There were muffled voices in the background, a harsh shushing, then silence. Carina could practically sense Sheila thinking.

"Carina," she finally said, and in those few syllables Carina heard her drop all the pretense. She spoke in the clipped voice that Carina had heard only a few times before, when Sheila wasn't aware that she was in earshot. In the past, Carina had considered it Sheila's "professional" voice. Now she realized it was just her real voice. "I understand that you don't know who to trust. But you need to know that I want to help you. I won't ask you why you think that Tanner—"

"Don't," Carina agreed. "Evidently I don't have a lot of time."

"But you're mistaken about one thing. The real threat to you right now is the Albanians. Not me. And they don't have the virus, there's no way they could have—"

"Don't insult me, Sheila," Carina snapped. "I'm not stupid. I saw the video. I know what the symptoms are. And I know why you did it too—because you want to force me to give you Uncle Walter's research."

"You actually think I'd risk your *life*?"

Carina laughed bitterly. "Nice try. You know, the worst thing about this is that Walter fell for your act. He left me a letter, you know. He said he trusted you for a long time. He *cared* about you."

"I can't—I don't even know where to begin to . . ." There was a pause, and then Sheila spoke more calmly. "I can have you picked up in moments. I have the antidote, enough for both of you, and you can be back to normal in an hour. The antidote is incredibly fast. It wipes all effects of the virus and leaves no footprint. I have to hand it to Walter—he really was a genius."

"Why'd you kill him, Sheila?" Carina asked. She couldn't stop herself. "I know he'd figured out how to manufacture and attach the antidote. Seems to me if you'd just stolen his data, you'd be selling out national security right now instead of talking to me."

Another pause, and when Sheila spoke again her voice had gone even emptier. "I didn't kill him. Sometimes I wanted to, especially when he suddenly decided to cut me out of research that I had been a part of from the start. I mean, Carina, Walter and your mother and I and dozens of other people have been working on this thing for years. Once we got close, all of a sudden he's the only one who gets to see it through to the end? The only one who gets to make decisions about the future of the project?"

"He just wanted it to be safe."

"Safe!" Sheila spat the word as if it were a curse. "*Safe* doesn't exist for people like him and me. We knew that when we signed on. Your mother knew it too. But you should know this: I didn't have anything to do with his death. And neither did the government. Ours, anyway."

"Then who did it? Let me guess, you thought you had everything you needed. Maybe you were afraid he'd want in on your little deal and you didn't want to share."

Sheila exhaled sharply in frustration. "Carina, listen to reason, let me help you—and that boyfriend of yours too. I'm the only person who can get you out of this alive. What else are you going to do, take your chances with your little computer genius when I'm offering you the resources of one of the most powerful research organizations in the world?" Her tone turned bitter. "I guess I've forgotten how powerful young love can be."

Carina pressed the end button.

Her heart raced with emotions, none more powerful than her fury at Sheila's last comment. Maybe because it was true. Carina *had* doomed Tanner, and it was love that had made her do it. Her grief had been overwhelming, once it sank in that Walter was never coming back. And Tanner had been there for her, his every word, every touch a comfort. She hadn't hesitated. She'd lost herself in his love and those few hours had made her stronger and kept her going, had made it possible for her to wake up the morning of her uncle's memorial service and know she would somehow get through it.

Tanner had saved her—but would it cost him his life?

"Did you hear all that?" she asked, trying to keep her voice steady.

"Most of it. Enough."

"I shouldn't have hung up on her. She's our only link to the antidote."

"You can always call her back, once we figure out a safer place to meet. I mean, we can't risk her coming here—even with all of Walter's protections, the minute we let them in the door, we're sitting ducks."

"But even if we figure out a better place to meet, I don't have anything to give her besides the key—and what if what she's looking for isn't in the locker? Uncle Walter never told me where his research is stored. I always assumed it was somewhere on the lab's servers."

"It probably was, until he decided it wasn't safe there. It could be anywhere—there's VPNs in a dozen different countries that could never be traced. Virtual private networks," he added automatically. Tanner was used to having to translate his computer terms for people. "You're sure he never gave you passwords, codes, anything?"

"Very sure. I mean ... one of the greatest things about him was that he was always direct. If there was something he wanted me to know, he just said it. But maybe that's what's stored in the locker, right? I mean, if Walter had wanted the research destroyed forever, he would have done that. But instead he wants to make sure the Army Criminal Investigation team or whatever it was called gets it. He must trust them to keep the virus out of the wrong hands."

"I had the same thought. And something else—Walter might have kept the antidote around, right? I mean, after seeing what was on that video ..." His voice trailed off, and Carina shuddered involuntarily. The images of the man attacking himself, blood running between his frantically claw-ing fingers, would not soon go away. "All I'm saying is that he must have kept a backup supply of the antidote some-where. And it isn't here."

"At least not where we can find it." She sighed. "He must have never dreamed I would need it."

"Or maybe he just couldn't bear to think about the pos-sibility. Even Walter's entitled to a little denial."

"Well ... we don't have many other options, right? If there's nothing in the locker that can help us, we can try to go to the lab. I might be able to figure out how to get into Walter's office, since it's not in the secure part of the build-ing." As she said it, though, she realized how unlikely it was that such a plan would work: the lab wasn't near a BART stop, and they didn't have a car. Carina knew where Uncle Walter kept his spare keys, but that would mean a trip to the house, which Sheila was undoubtedly having watched. And besides, the lab used fingerprint recognition at most of the entrances, even the nonsecure office wing. "But if it gets close to thirty-six hours, we're going to have to throw ourselves on Sheila's mercy."

"No. It's not going to get that far. After we check the locker, if there's nothing there, we call that Major Wynnside guy. Maybe he can do something. Find Sheila, or someone else at the lab, force them to produce the antidote...."

"Yeah, sure," Carina agreed readily, but she knew they were both thinking the same thing: that would take time. Even if the major had all the resources of the armed ser-vices at his disposal, finding Sheila and forcing her to give them what they wanted—especially since they were working from inside the system, unlike the rogue agents who'd killed Walter—would take too long to save them.

"Okay." She took a deep breath and ran her fingers through her newly shorn hair. "I guess it's time to go."

≪◆≫

It was only two BART stops to the Civic Center station. Carina and Tanner slouched in seats at opposite ends of the nearly empty car, trying to look bored. Carina's legs had begun to jitter uncontrollably, and she tried to force them to be still by pressing down on them without drawing attention to herself. Tanner had the backpack containing the laptop, disposable phone, and money, and as much of the nonperishable food and water as he had been able to jam in the pack. Carina had the letter and keys in a pocket of her shorts. She scanned the other riders, unable to stop feeling like they were watching her. If a Calaveras Lab security team had suddenly burst through the doors between the cars, she wouldn't have been surprised.

It was almost one in the morning. Some of the passengers looked like they were returning from second-shift jobs, dozing or listening to music—Carina could hear it clearly even through their earbuds, the many small sounds in the car competing inside her head. Other passengers looked like they'd been partying, dressed up for an evening out, and she could detect half a dozen different perfumes.

The Civic Center station was relatively empty, the

booths shuttered, trash skittering along the stained concrete floor as the train rushed down the track. Carina and Tanner followed the signs to the long bank of lockers deep within the underground station. No one else was in the corridor.

"I'll go," Carina said as they stared down the empty hall. Her heart was hammering in her chest. "You stay here. If anything happens . . . Tanner, you have to run, seriously."

"You're out of your mind." He smiled when he said it, but Carina had no doubt he was serious. "You're my ticket to fame and fortune."

If they'd had more time, she might have argued. Instead, she approached the locker warily, looking for anything out of place. It was one of the smaller ones, near the top, and her hand shook as she slid in the key.

It turned easily. Nothing happened: no explosion burst from the small space. Carina wasn't sure what she had been expecting, but as she reached inside, she felt great relief nonetheless.

An envelope. Her name in Walter's handwriting. It was becoming a treasure hunt, like the ones Emma's mother had set up every year for Emma's birthday when they were little. All around town, Mrs. Choi hid clues in places like the ice cream shop and the post office, concluding the search with cake and balloons in the park. How Carina had envied Emma, who never seemed to understand how lucky she was. On Carina's birthday, her mother usually gave her a gift certificate, a practice she'd started before Carina was old enough to go shopping by herself.

Carina shook her head to push away the memory. There

was something else in the locker: a small device that looked a little like a car remote, with a display flashing a series of numbers. She handed it to Tanner, who examined it carefully. "I think this—"

He was interrupted by the sound of footsteps echoing around the corner. Running.

Tanner jammed the device in his pocket and grabbed her hand. "Run!"

Carina glanced over her shoulder as she pivoted and took off. Black jackets. Short hair. The stone-faced expressions of the two muscular young men matched those of every Calaveras Lab security team member, even if she couldn't identify these two. But she was sure they wouldn't stop until they caught Carina and Tanner one way or another.

They careened down the corridor, bland cinder-block walls flashing by. Carina was aware of her lungs filling with air, her muscles stretching and flexing, her heart pumping blood through her veins. But now, knowing that her body was playing host to a virus that heightened her senses and increased her strength, it was almost as though she were seeing herself from another dimension. She anticipated her feet hitting the floor with perfect precision. She felt the arc of her arms' motion both in real time and, somehow, in slow motion, envisioning their perfect concordance. She willed herself to lengthen her strides, to cover more distance, and she could sense the thousands of tiny adjustments, brain to nerves and muscles, that made it happen. And beside her, Tanner was keeping pace, his own form flawless.

As horrifying as it was to know that she had been injected with a deadly substance, and despite the fact that she was being pursued by armed gunmen, it was exhilarating to push her body to its limits. Down a flight of stairs, through another corridor, past signs indicating an exit up onto Hyde Street. There it was, the turnstile that led to freedom, and their pursuers had fallen behind; she couldn't even hear their footsteps. Carina skidded to a stop, Tanner doing the same beside her. The turnstile was a spinning column of steel bars, eight feet tall—and it was chained and padlocked.

USE GROVE ST. EXIT AFTER 9 P.M. M–F read a sign looped through the chain.

Now she heard the footsteps, quickly gaining on them.

Tanner grabbed the bars and pushed, making a guttural sound of frustration, and as Carina watched, he actually managed to bend two of the bars. She couldn't begin to imagine how much force it would take to bend steel, but it wasn't going to help since there was no way the thing was turning while the chain was on.

"Tanner, stop!" she shouted, grabbing his arm. "We need to figure—"

She stopped abruptly as the two men came into view, holding weapons, aiming as they ran. Darts again, presumably, though Carina was sure that by now they'd adjusted the dose to account for the virus, and whatever they shot her with would make her drop like a stone. And what about Tanner? There was no reason for them to be careful with him.

"... heading south, blocked at exit," she heard one of them bark into his wrist, and then an all-too-familiar voice screaming at them to hurry. Even through the static Carina could tell it was Sheila, and the hairs on her neck stood up. How could she ever have trusted her?

"Hang on," Tanner muttered, turning to the trash can pushed up against the wall. The top, made of metal, was a domed shell that covered the can and kept the plastic liner in place. Tanner ripped it off.

The motion spun him, his own strength giving him momentum. A ping sounded, and Carina knew that one of their pursuers had fired and almost hit Tanner with a dart. Instinctively she ducked and pressed herself against the wall. A second dart whizzed past, inches from her shoulder. If it hadn't been for her almost preternatural responsiveness, she would have been hit.

Fear segued to anger. Carina was growing tired of being pursued and shot at by people who didn't even know her. As Tanner dipped one shoulder in the elegant, graceful motion that she knew was the windup to his discus throw, she turned and ran directly at the closer man.

Tanner spun and released, the can lid leaving his hand at the same moment that the man took aim at her. Carina heard a growling scream that she realized was coming from her own throat as the man began to squeeze the trigger. She was able to see the twitch of his finger even though he was ten feet away, as though her vision were being sharpened and magnified inside her mind, and as she braced to be hit, her momentum too great to veer away, there was a loud crash and he was knocked sideways, the lid connecting with his torso.

He grunted in pain and dropped the gun. It went off when it hit the floor, the dart striking the ceiling. Tanner had run at an angle, and as the other guard tried to take aim, Carina saw him bank off the wall, running halfway up the side until his body was parallel to the floor. Carina dove for the gun, absorbing the impact and letting it carry her along. She slid right past the first man, who was doubled over, moaning. The gun was small, short-barreled, and lightweight in her hand; she jammed it into the pocket of her shorts as she scrambled to her feet.

Tanner landed, as light as a panther. The guard was clutching his face, staggering toward them. She could hear Sheila's voice coming through the device on his wrist, demanding to know their status.

"What did you do to him?" Carina asked as they ran back the way they'd come.

"Kicked him in the mouth," Tanner said. "Not much finesse, but it worked."

Carina was trying to figure out how his foot had connected with an object—a man's face—that was five feet off the ground. He must have managed a kick as he came off the wall, a maneuver requiring such precision that Carina would have thought it impossible.

Of course, *none* of what they'd just done ought to have been possible. Their strength, speed, agility, all of it was artificial. Biochemical.

And all of it would cause her insides to deteriorate in just a few short hours.

She ran faster.

CHAPTER TEN

Saturday, 1:48 a.m.
04:11:06

Two blocks from the BART station, City Hall rose up into the inky sky. The wide, grassy park in front of it was host to a few other people, despite the hour: homeless men and women huddling on benches and sleeping on sidewalks, a few drunks staggering along with their bottles gripped tightly.

Tanner and Carina had stopped to take a drink of water at a bench under a row of flags that flapped in the breeze.

"We ought to be freezing," Carina said. She touched her arms and her skin was chilly, but inside, her heart was pushing blood through her system so efficiently that she felt warm. The tics were worsening; she could feel the twitching all over her body, like little electric currents were being applied to her skin. Exertion quelled them temporarily, but as soon as she stopped running, they started up again.

And they would only get worse.

"I'm hungry again," Tanner replied. He dug in the pack and pulled out a couple of energy bars and a bottle of water. They ate and drank in silence, wolfing down the tasteless food, which barely took the edge off Carina's hunger.

"At least we know one thing," she said, after taking a deep drink from the water bottle. "You were right about the tracker on your phone. I can't believe they didn't get us at the apartment."

"No." Tanner shook his head. "It would have taken them a while. The bottleneck would have been in finding my number. I mean, I still can't believe they were able to move that fast. You know how hard it is to get access to those records? They would have had to have access to the cell phone provider's internal database, and there are so many levels of encryption on it that they would have had to get in a different way."

"You mean—someone from inside was helping them?"

"Or someone powerful enough to get people out of bed requisitioned the records."

"But who could do that? I mean . . . are you thinking it's government?"

"I'm not thinking anything," Tanner said, holding up his hands in protest. "Other than it's someone with a scary amount of power."

"Or someone with influence. Or money."

"It keeps coming back to that, doesn't it? Makes your

head spin. Here." He reached into the backpack and handed her the note from the locker.

"Again?" Carina sighed. "I feel like this is getting a little stupid. I mean, I wish Walter had just talked to me instead of leading us all over town."

"He was trying to protect you. The less you knew ... I mean, if everything hadn't gotten so screwed up, you might have always believed they were working on some harmless nutrition project, and you could have gone on to live the perfect high school senior year."

"Yeah," Carina mumbled.

She opened the envelope and took out the note. At least this time there was no key, no cryptic next step. Smoothing the paper on her lap, she began to read using the streetlight above them.

My dear Carrie,

If you are reading this, then I must assume I am dead or as good as dead, and that things are dire. No plan is foolproof, and as I made these preparations, I had to consider what would happen if you were not able to bring the major in to help you. This is a terrible turn of events, but in recent months I've learned that things can always get worse. So now we must both focus on helping you survive.

And that means that I have to share a secret that I have kept faithfully

during this last year. Your mother is
alive, Carrie. I know this is shocking
news and you must be very angry at me
for keeping it from you, but please
bear with me. Right now you MUST focus
on your own safety.

Carina let out an involuntary gasp. "My mother—"
But Tanner took the paper from her. He read the rest
aloud.

Over a year ago, soon after we'd
finally created an antidote, your
mother came to me and said she
suspected someone was leaking data,
that they were selling our work to
someone outside the lab. She had
already shared her concerns with
Calaveras management, not wanting
to involve me if she was wrong.
When they dismissed her inquiry,
she threatened to take her concerns
to the FBI, and suddenly she began
receiving threats on her life. Always
anonymous, always untraceable, but
she was convinced they were coming
from someone on the inside at the lab.
I thought she was being paranoid,
exaggerating or maybe even imagining
these threats. I had personally
vetted everyone on our team, every
technician, every research assistant,

even our administrative staff, the
custodians. I never once thought to
suspect Sheila.

But then Madelyn disappeared, and
her suicide note was found. Several
people called to say they'd seen her
on the bridge that night—people will
say anything, I guess, especially if a
suggestion has been planted in their
minds by the media. But a few days
after her memorial, she called me.
Nearly gave me a heart attack. I was
desperate to find her, I begged her to
come back, if only for you, but she
said that she had to keep pretending
she was dead—that if 'they' knew she
was alive they'd go after me. She
believed the only way to keep *you* safe
was to pretend she was dead, because
they could use you to get to her. She
gave me a phone number to use only for
emergencies, and she said that if I
told anyone she was alive, she would
disappear forever and I'd never hear
from her again. I still didn't believe
her. I thought maybe she was having
some sort of breakdown, but I didn't
know what to do.

And now it turns out that she was
right all along. Sheila was peddling
our work to the highest bidder, and she
is every bit as ruthless as your mother
believed. I no longer know who is

innocent and who is working with her,
but I don't trust anyone.

It was very hard to keep your
mother's existence secret, but I did
as she asked. I am so sorry, Carrie,
but I didn't know what else to do. I've
talked to her a few times in the past
year, always when she calls me. She is
safe, and I know she will do everything
she can to keep you safe too.

I love you, Carrie.
—Uncle Walter

Carina realized she had stopped breathing. Tanner handed the letter back to her. She folded it carefully and slipped it back into the envelope, her hands trembling.

"My mother ...," she started, but her voice broke. "I can't believe this."

"Car ..." Tanner hugged her. "I mean, this is ... amazing."

"Amazing?" A surge of anger took hold of Carina, the strength of it making her squeeze her fists and clench her teeth. She could feel the blood vessels in her neck pulsing, and she forced herself to take a deep breath, tremors racking her body. "Amazing that a mother could go an entire year without ever talking to her daughter? Knowing what she was going through, knowing—"

Tanner held her tighter as a sob escaped her throat. "It's okay, Car, it's okay," he murmured, her tears spilling onto his chest.

"She had to know how much I missed her. How devastated I was."

"She was trying to *protect* you. Look, you have to call her now. She must have some of the antidote, and now she can help you. Don't you see how she's been waiting for this moment? She had to be praying it would never come, and also desperate to see you again."

Carina swallowed, trying to process what she had just learned. "I—I just can't believe she let me think she was dead, all this time." She twisted the ring on her finger, the points of the hexagonal stone sharp against her skin. Her mother—*alive*. How many times following her funeral had Carina cried herself to sleep, thinking about the last conversations they'd had, all the opportunities she'd missed to tell her she loved her? How often had she felt the ache of her absence like a burning hole in her heart that she could never reveal? And the whole time, her mother had never reached out to her to reassure her, to explain why she had disappeared, to tell her she missed her. Even to hear her voice.

But there wasn't time for that now. She took the phone and dialed the number scrawled at the bottom of the note.

It rang twice before it was answered, the voice on the other end so familiar it brought tears to Carina's eyes.

"Mom. It's me."

It took a few minutes to hail a cab, but when Tanner pushed some bills at the driver, he put the pedal to the floor.

The address Madelyn had given her was in a working-class neighborhood fifteen minutes from the center of the city. Since it was the middle of the night, the cabbie said he could make it in ten.

Carina rested her head against Tanner's chest, even though she didn't feel the least bit tired. The jittery sensations that had been plaguing her nerves had increased, until it felt like an electric current had completed the circuit within her, sparking along her synapses. She had to remind herself to blink, but then at other times her eyelids would spasm, fluttering out of control. Even after sharing a bottle of water with Tanner, her mouth felt dry. She felt like walking—no, running—if only to channel some of the extra energy away from her muscles.

Instead, she nestled into Tanner's arms and listened to his heartbeat. It was fast, too fast, but it was also soothing. She inhaled his scent, and it was amazingly clear, as though all the individual notes—laundry detergent, soap, fabric softener, sweat—were tangled into a knot that she could untie with her mind.

"Think about next year," Tanner said, rubbing her back. "In six months you'll be just another college freshman with a bad haircut."

Carina knew he was trying to distract her, to take her mind off the reunion that lay ahead, but she couldn't force herself to go along, because her mind was beginning to go haywire along with her body. Tanner's infection was several hours behind hers; soon enough he would feel what she was feeling, thoughts starting to fray at the edges. It was becoming difficult to concentrate—and impossible to lie. "But I won't be with you," she said miserably, her voice almost lost in the sound of the cabbie's scratchy radio, the wind rushing through the open windows, the traffic noise.

Tanner's hands went still on her back. They'd circled this discussion so many times. About Tanner's acceptance to Berkeley, and all of the rejections Carina received before her acceptance to Cal State Long Beach.

Before Madelyn died, Carina had performed well in all of her classes. But afterward, her grades tanked and she never recovered. Looking back now, she had to admit that her mother's death had created a deep chasm of grief, loss, and loneliness that nothing could fill. Schoolwork wasn't hard for Carina—just pointless, at least when all she had to look forward to was an empty house and the take-out dinners her uncle would bring home long after everyone else had left the office.

All those nights, she'd ignored the textbooks stacked up on her desk and spent time on Facebook or watching shows on Netflix or working on problems in her cryptography books. She went out with her friends, and learned how to hide the emptiness, but she never forgot she was the only one with virtually no family. Being part of the track team had helped, though sometimes she used the workouts to make herself so tired that she could fall asleep without having to think.

When Tanner came along, everything changed. Carina began to believe in a future. She started to see the outline of a family she could build for herself, one made up of friends, people who loved her, with Tanner at the center of it all.

But it wasn't enough. The plummeting of her GPA meant she didn't qualify for Berkeley, one of the toughest schools in the country to get into. She celebrated along with her friends when Emma was accepted at Michigan and Nikki got into Sonoma State. When her own acceptance letter came from Cal State Long Beach, she was grateful for the opportunity.

But Tanner wouldn't be there.

They'd only talked about it twice, and both times Carina had cut the conversation short. Because there was only one way it could work out, and that was with them being separated. Sure, they could see each other on weekends sometimes, maybe holidays, depending on when their breaks were. But Carina had gotten used to seeing Tanner almost every day. She had needed to see him, almost like she needed oxygen, even before Walter's death. Now he was all she had. And if they lived through the day, she wasn't sure she could bear to be apart.

"You can't think that way, Car," Tanner whispered into her hair.

"But what other—"

"This the street?" the cabbie asked, his voice making Carina jump. It was impossibly loud inside the car, a trick of her heightened senses.

She looked out the window and understood why he was dubious. They were driving slowly up a steep incline, a narrow street that was full of potholes. Cracked sidewalks gave way to driveways crammed with beat-up cars. The houses looked shabby, a few of them boarded up and covered with graffiti.

"Um, is this Mortimer Street?"

"Yes, miss."

"Then I guess . . . yes, that's number 165."

The cabbie pulled over and Tanner handed over some bills. They got out of the cab, Tanner shrugging the backpack over his shoulders, and regarded the house, a battered two-story structure that was missing several shutters. The porch railing hung loose off broken posts, and a single lamp glowed behind dingy curtains. Carina made no move toward the house, letting Tanner hold her instead; she wasn't sure if she was shaking all over because she was about to see her mother for the first time in almost a year, or because the virus was wreaking further havoc on her nervous system.

"So she said she has the antidote, right?" Tanner asked.

"Yes." The truth was, her mother had started crying and it was hard to understand what she was saying. Carina had given her mother an abbreviated version of everything that had happened in the last day, from being chased from the cemetery to finding Walter's apartment to being attacked at the BART station. Madelyn had begged her to come straight to her house.

"Car . . . before we go in, I need to tell you something," Tanner said. "I think I know what that thing is. From the locker."

He took it out of her pocket, but it was too dark to examine it outside the house, since the display was not backlit. "You barely got a look at it."

"Didn't need to. I saw it flash the codes. My guess is that it's generating them every few seconds."

"What, like, randomly?"

"Sort of, except it's mirroring a sequence on a server. It's an ever-changing password for a specific gateway, and while it could be anywhere, I think it's wherever your uncle stored his research backup."

Tanner started to unzip the backpack's outer pocket, then stopped and crouched down. "I wonder ... Yeah, it fits, just barely."

"Your *sock*? Seriously?" Tanner had found running socks with a zipped pocket on the Internet, and he wore them to train in because they held his keys. They were the only socks he ever wore, even today, with the clothes he'd worn to the funeral.

"Well, look at it this way: you've got the ring with the IP address, I've got the token generator. Even if something happens to the backpack, we're covered."

Carina had to admit it made sense. Without the token generator and the ring, they had nothing. Walter had destroyed the lab's access to the data—and in the process, Sheila's. "Why didn't he just destroy it all? I mean, if he thought it was that dangerous, why not delete every copy, every backup? Make it so no one could ever find it?"

"But that's the problem, Car. They can re-create the *virus*. They just can't re-create the antidote, at least the version that's attached to the virus itself, so you can't be infected without it—the foolproof version."

"So ... if Walter destroyed it, they could have more accidents like the one we saw in the video—"

"That was no accident, Car—they left that poor guy there to die, and kept the camera rolling. That was an experiment, and he was their guinea pig."

"Okay, right, so Walter figured if he destroyed his research, Sheila would just sell the virus as is, without giving any thought to the consequences. That's why he was going to contact Major Wynnside—he trusted the Army Criminal Investigation Command to stop her, and if the lab went forward with the project after that, at least they'd be able to produce a virus that was safe to use."

"And that's where that password generator comes in—to get into his private files on the VPN."

"But how does the password on that thing match up to the one on the server? I mean you said it could be anywhere on earth—"

"Yeah, but— Look, Car, it'll take me too long to explain it now. The reason I brought it up is, when we go in there, I think you need to, uh, maybe not mention it to your mom."

"Why wouldn't I tell her? Tanner, she was the one who tried to stop this project from the start."

"Um, yeah. I mean, that's what Walter thought."

"You don't believe him?" Carina felt her chest tighten. "You don't trust my mom?"

"Look, Car, I never met her. I believe what you've told me about her," Tanner said hastily. "But, you know, there are a lot of players here and not a lot of time to get this right, and I just thought, it wouldn't hurt to hold back a little until we have the injection."

Carina pulled away from him, shocked that he suspected her mother could be capable of betraying them. But what if it was true? How well had she really known her mother? How many times had she wished they were closer, that her mother confided in her, asked her about her day—cared about her the way mothers were supposed to care about their children?

"Just—just let me have this one thing, okay? Let me have this time with my mom, without ruining it?" Carina dug her fingers into her palm, something she often did when she was upset—and nearly yelped with pain. Uncurling her fingers, she held her hand up and saw the dark runnels in the middle—she'd drawn her own blood.

Tanner took her hand and examined it under the weak light from the streetlamps, turning it over. "Damn, Carina—" He lifted the corner of his shirt and gently dabbed at the blood.

The gesture was so tender that Carina couldn't think of anything to say. She felt like she was getting worse; it was hard to control her strength, her impulses. And she had to admit that at least some of the anger she was feeling toward Tanner was misplaced. It would be so much easier to lash out at him than to face the faint doubts that she also had. "I won't tell her about the password generator," she said, keeping her face as neutral as she could.

"And maybe the computer . . . you know, until we're sure."

Carina's jaw clenched. "Maybe *you* should trust *me* a little more. I'm willing to wait and see, but, Tanner, if I feel like she's being honest with me, after she gives us the antidote, you can't stop me from telling her everything."

"I know I can't stop you, Car," Tanner said, anger edging

into his voice too. "And I've *always* trusted you. I think it's pretty damn ironic that you're accusing me of anything else. I thought you finally understood that I'm not the enemy. That I lo—"

"Stop." Carina's voice sounded frantic, even to her. She knew what he was going to say—and she couldn't deal with it. Couldn't stand to hear it, especially now. Love wasn't something she was ready to acknowledge out loud, no matter how right it felt to be with Tanner, no matter what sort of thoughts she had whenever he was near, no matter how often she fantasized about them being together next month, next year. "Please just don't. I mean, not now. My *mom* is in there, and I—"

"I understand," Tanner said grimly, cutting her off and backing away from her with his palms raised. "I do. But think about this—we're in a hell of a bad situation here, and we may not have a lot of tomorrows ahead of us. So if you're ever going to get around to facing the way I know you feel about me, you might want to start soon."

With that he strode up to the door and started pounding, leaving Carina to hurry up the walk after him. The door opened almost as soon as he knocked, the figure behind it obscured in the unlit room beyond.

"Get in here quick," the familiar voice said. "Oh, Carina, it really is you."

CHAPTER ELEVEN

Saturday, 2:31 a.m.
03:28:24

When the door shut behind them a light turned on, almost blinding Carina as she threw herself into her mother's arms.

"Mom! Oh my God, I can't believe it. I can't . . ." She inhaled her mother's familiar scent, her shampoo and perfume, as Madelyn hugged her hard. She was thinner, and she had let her hair grow long, but it was still the same rich red that it had always been.

Her mother had never been the hugging type; it had been one of the things that had made it so hard for Carina after her death. Everyone wanted to comfort her in the weeks following the funeral, and they had showered her with affection. People from the lab, her friends' mothers, they enveloped her in big, comforting hugs. Even Walter was more affectionate than Madelyn had ever been. And it had taken a while for Carina to get used to it, when all she wanted was the quick back-patting embraces her mother had given her from time to time.

But now her mother held on like she would never let go. Finally, she released Carina, hands on her shoulders, her eyes filled with emotion. "Look at you! Oh, Carina, you're so ... I mean ... oh, how I've missed you. I thought, I just thought I would never see you again. I almost couldn't bear it. And then Walter—" She swiped at her eyes, smudging her mascara, wiping away tears. "I'm sorry, honey. This is your friend, yes? Hello, Tanner."

She offered her hand and Tanner shook it. "It's nice to meet you, Mrs. Monroe."

"Come with me. Back this way. Away from the windows." She led them into the house, which was furnished with shabby, nondescript furniture. Carina looked around as they passed through the living room and saw no personal effects, no photographs. She couldn't help feeling disappointed that there were no pictures of her anywhere. But maybe that was her mother's way of protecting her. Maybe she couldn't have pictures because she was always looking over her shoulder, worrying that she was one misstep away from being found. From meeting the same fate Walter had—for real this time.

"Was that you who called us, Mom?" Carina guessed. "Back at the apartment?"

"Yes. You can't imagine how worried I've been. I had a friend of mine watching the memorial service—when he reported that you'd disappeared with Sheila's security detail after you, I was praying you'd make it to Walter's safe room."

"And I hung up on you?" Carina asked, horrified. "But why did you disguise your voice?"

"Baby, I was just trying to protect you. I still thought the way to keep you safe was to never let you find out about me. But I just had to know. I should never have called. It was so stupid of me—I should have known how upset you would be, and I only made things worse. I'm so sorry."

"I just—I never dreamed—" Carina's voice faltered as they reached the kitchen. "How did you do it, Mom? How'd you disappear?"

Madelyn took Carina's hand, her eyes glittering with tears. "Sweetheart, I could have never done it without the help of a few trusted friends, and— Oh! You're wearing the ring! Did you ever . . ."

"Find the secret inside? Yes, I did. And Walter left me the cryptographic token."

"I had a feeling he would, if he ever thought he was under any threat." Madelyn sighed. "I know it was a risk, but I just thought . . . I couldn't bear not to have any connection to you. And this way, I thought if anything happened to both me and Walter, there would still be one person in the world who had access to our work. To the research that could be used to create an antidote. So that if the virus ever was used, at least there was a way to keep it from killing innocent people."

"But what if I'd never found it?"

"I guess . . ." Madelyn spoke quietly, not meeting Carina's eyes. "I thought if it was ever meant to be, you'd find it."

"That's pretty unscientific, isn't it?" Carina said, surprised.

Madelyn looked embarrassed. "Yes. I suppose it is. But

you know, if I've learned one thing in the last year, it's that I let science take over too much of my life. I gave time to my work that I should have spent with you. I—I hope you won't make the same mistake."

"Mrs. Monroe, I know Carina has already told you this over the phone, but we really need the antidote," Tanner said apologetically. "I mean, I think we'll all feel more relaxed, and we can think about the next steps. It's getting—well, I guess you probably know what's happening. We don't have a lot of time."

"It's been about thirty-three hours," Carina said. "I've only got three hours left before ..."

She couldn't bear to complete the thought, especially after seeing her mother blanch with fear.

"We'll go in a minute," Madelyn said. "I just need to make sure you weren't followed here."

"Go? Go where?" The edge in Tanner's voice was more pronounced.

"This isn't where I live," Madelyn said. She took Carina's hand in hers and squeezed it hard, never taking her eyes off her. Carina understood—she had an urge to grab her mother and hang on, to keep her close now that she had found her. "I do some of the time. I have three places I use. We'll head over to where I have supplies. Walter insisted on giving me the antidote when it was ready—he sent it to an unmarked PO box I use. It may have lost a little effectiveness, but it will still be plenty potent."

"Mom, I wish—I don't—" Carina's thoughts and wishes tumbled together, and she could voice none of them. What she'd pretended for so long—that love was impossible for her—it was a lie; the love she'd had for her distant and pre-occupied mother had never been destroyed, the way she had made herself believe. It had just been buried, and now that her mother was here in the flesh, warm and breathing and clutching her hand, she dared to long for more. If they could just get through this, find the antidote and contact the major, then maybe they could stay in contact. Maybe there was a way to be together again someday, a way to build their lives around each other. Carina couldn't help feeling a surge of hope that they would live long enough for her mother to see her graduate, to enter college, all the milestones Carina had thought she would have to endure alone.

"Hush," Madelyn said, squeezing her hand. "I know. I know. Leaving you was the hardest thing I ever did, but I was afraid that if I didn't back off they would hurt you. So I decided to make it seem that I was gone forever. Oh, Carina, I would have hated myself for putting you in danger, and I swore to myself I wouldn't allow you to be involved in any way, even if that meant I never saw you. The risks were too great. I wished I'd never said anything, even though I knew what could happen if the virus got out."

"But you told Walter . . ."

"As soon as I told him what I suspected, he figured out the rest. He was always smarter than me." A small, sad smile played at her lips. "There. I said it. How he would have loved to hear that."

"But you were the only one who went to the management?"

"Yes. We thought, because we knew there was a risk, that

they would fire the person who questioned what was going on. We were sure they would suspect a leak, and the lab can't take that kind of a hit on its reputation. So we believed that this way, even if I was fired, Walter would still be able to keep working on the antidote. And if we couldn't stop the virus from getting out into the world, we could at least make it safer for people." While she spoke, she had been gathering her purse and keys. "Now let's get moving."

"You can tell us the rest on the way," Carina said.

"Yes. Yes, that's best. Carina, I'm so sorry for all the time I spent away from you," Madelyn said, her voice hitching. She sat down and took Carina's hand. "Oh, sweetheart, if only I could do it all over again . . ."

The sound of glass breaking interrupted her, and Carina's attention snapped to the kitchen window, where one of the panes had shattered. Tanner was already on his feet, launching himself at Carina as she turned back to her mother. It all was happening in slow motion because there, against the pale knit fabric of her mother's shirt, was a tiny, neat hole that was blossoming into a red-petaled flower. As Tanner's hands grasped Carina's shoulders and pushed her toward the floor, she saw her mother slowly slip down in her chair, a look of surprise in her eyes.

When they hit the floor, Carina was still holding her mother's hand. Blood poured from the hole in her chest, and her pulse was weakening under her warm skin. Someone screamed, a long, keening sound of grief, and it was only when Tanner clamped his hand over Carina's mouth that she realized it was her.

"Car, no, stop, you have to stop," he hissed in her ear as he tried to drag her away. "Please, listen, we have to get out of here."

Carina fought him, pushing and scratching. His back hit the bank of cabinets and he let out an *oof* and Carina knew she'd pushed him too hard but she had to get to her mother, had to try to save her. She pressed her hand to her mother's cheek, feeling her eyelids flutter. Her mother's lips trembled, and then she whispered her name.

"Carina . . . baby, I love you. Go. Go. . . ."

Tanner scrambled across the kitchen and hit the light switch, casting them into darkness, and her mother pushed her away weakly.

Carina had lost her mother once before, but this time it was for real. Tanner dragged her to her feet and toward the doorway just as a second crash sent more glass splintering from the back door.

"This way!" Tanner yelled, pulling her back toward the front of the house. But Carina saw something—no, that wasn't entirely right, especially since it was dark outside the windows and the drapes were drawn all the way. But she sensed something, perhaps a change in the air currents, or a sound too small to be picked up by human ears.

But not by *super*human ears. Because wasn't that what she and Tanner now possessed? The ability to sense things others couldn't sense? And why shouldn't that include danger?

There wasn't time to scream, wasn't time to explain. She

pulled Tanner to the side, away from the path to the door and toward the stairs, and he seemed to understand because he corrected his course and hit the bottom step running.

The front door was battered by something enormous and loud, but there wasn't time to look. Carina and Tanner raced up the stairs, into a dim hall that stank of mildew. Carina chose a direction at random and prayed she'd picked right. Heading for the door at the end of the hall, she hit it head-on, with Tanner at her side. She'd have a hell of a bruise on her shoulder if she survived this night, but the door splintered. Tanner kicked the broken board twice, and a section of the wood clattered to the floor.

They had run *through* the door.

There was something deeply unsettling about that, Carina thought as they ran the obstacle course of the bedroom, around a bed covered with an ancient chenille spread, ducking past an armoire with sagging doors, toward the window that faced the side of the house. You shouldn't be able to run through a solid piece of wood, but they had broken a hole in it. Her shoulder tingled, but it didn't hurt, exactly, or if it did, she was sensing pain in a whole new way.

Tanner reached the window first and yanked at the brass handle on the sash. It creaked but didn't budge. Carina grasped the other handle and pulled, the fittings popping and flying into the air as the window shot up. She thought for sure the glass would break, but it only shuddered as she heard shouting and the crash of things being shoved or thrown aside on the floor below them.

"Go," Tanner hissed, and Carina didn't have to be told twice. She let herself out the window onto the sloping roof just as Tanner added, "Oh shit."

She knew she shouldn't stop, even for a split second, but she couldn't help it. She turned and looked past Tanner, who was scrambling through the opening as fast as he could, and found herself staring at a man lurching through the door of the room.

A beard. None of the security team at the lab had beards, she thought just as the man pulled the trigger on the ugly black handgun he'd leveled at Tanner and the report echoed around the room.

"Uh," Tanner said as he dropped lightly to the roof. Carina gasped.

"Are you hit?"

"No. Go."

She skittered down the incline; there wasn't time to be careful, and if she slid she wouldn't have time to correct her course before she hit the concrete below, and she'd break a bone, or worse. But when she got to the gutter, thankful for the traction from the rubber soles of her shoes, she grabbed its metal edge in one hand and swung out into the air.

For a second she held on by one hand, trying to calculate how to hit the softer dirt rather than the sidewalk; then Tanner let go and landed in a graceful crouch and she realized it didn't matter.

She *hoped* it didn't matter, anyway, and in the small amount of time it took for her to free-fall the dozen or so feet, she was able to complete the perplexing thought that she was becoming entirely too comfortable with her super-powers.

Though what did it matter? She'd just lost both her mother—again—and her best chance at getting the antidote before her time ran out.

CHAPTER TWELVE

Saturday, 3:08 a.m.
02:51:36

Her feet hit the concrete and the shock traveled through her body as though in a stop-motion sequence, Carina making tiny adjustments to her balance and stance to compensate. When she straightened up again she was fine.

Tanner was rubbing his thigh, yelling at her to follow him. Only, when his hand came away from his shorts, she saw that it was covered with blood.

"Oh my God, you've been shot!"

"Barely, Car, it's nothing. Come on!"

But they'd hesitated a second too long. A shout from above drew their attention to the roof they'd just escaped from; there, framed in the window, was the bearded man. He took a shot but it went wild, and as he crawled onto the roof and prepared to fire again, a second man burst through the window.

He was enormous, completely bald, his teeth glinting in the moonlight. And he didn't look like he planned on stopping as he crab-walked down the roof. His progress was awkward because of the gun he was holding, a big two-handed-grip model like you saw in news reports about gangs, the kind of automatic weapon that could cut down several victims at a time.

Carina didn't need any more encouragement. She ran, Tanner close behind, as the big man reached the edge of the roof and the other man began firing again.

The street led down the hill to a valley laid out like a glittering grid. At three in the morning, South San Francisco, a working-class area of the city, was fast asleep, indifferent to the drama going on above. Carina watched for porch lights turning on, people investigating the sound of shooting, but no one stirred. Shops, closed for the night, were interspersed with block after block of densely packed, shabby little houses like the one her mother had been staying in. Any hope they had of escaping through the backyards uphill was dashed by the presence of a huge sound wall behind the homes.

"This way!" Carina shouted as she turned left, then ran down a cracked-asphalt driveway and into the backyard of a house across the street. She hoped they would encounter fences or other obstacles that would hinder their pursuers but that she and Tanner could vault. But most of the houses were separated by nothing more than trash-littered alleys and low picket fences that wouldn't stop a child, much less two heavily armed men. Worse, Tanner's wound had slowed him down; he ran with a crooked gait, favoring his left leg. The backpack had slid off one of his shoulders, half pinning his arm. He might not even be able to clear a fence, depending on how badly he was injured.

"Go! Don't wait for me!" he said, trying to push her away.

"No!"

She took his hand and pulled him along. She'd left her mother only because there was no way to get her out of the house without dooming themselves. She would not leave Tanner. Carina could hear the men shouting at each other and realized they were speaking something that sounded almost like Russian. *Albanian.*

Carina's blood ran cold. So it was true. No matter what else Sheila had lied about, she hadn't lied about the rogue mafia, the deadly Albanians; now she and Tanner were being pursued by men who wanted them dead. If they just waited another day, Carina and Tanner would oblige them by dying from the virus.

But she didn't plan on giving them the satisfaction.

Carina veered around a corner, past a little bungalow festooned with clotheslines, and into a street that led to the bottom of the hill. A car passed, and Carina considered trying to flag it down, but in the second before she threw herself into the street to get the driver's attention, she realized that men willing to shoot at two unarmed teenagers probably wouldn't hesitate to add an adult bystander to the list of casualties. And there was no way she could explain the danger fast enough to convince someone to be their getaway driver. They could all end up being killed.

The car traveled up the hill, its taillights disappearing when it went over the crest. Carina was left trying to choose between several poor possibilities. Straight ahead, the road passed over a small, mostly dried-up creek before entering a commercial area, the next block anchored by an auto body shop and a shuttered corner grocery. To the right and left were side streets much like the ones they'd already passed: shabby little houses, cars parked along the curbs, trash cans at the street. The residents of the neighborhood slept on, oblivious to the drama unfolding just blocks away.

Tanner was loping toward the auto body shop, grimacing from the pain every time the foot on his injured leg struck pavement. "Over here!" he shouted. "We might be able to find cover."

Carina followed him past the locked entrance and a rusting vending machine, and into the parking lot separating the shop from the building next to it, a strip mall that smelled of garbage and fried food. She focused on Tanner, anxiously watching the blooming bloodstain on his shorts.

Then Tanner stopped short and she almost crashed into him. Looking up, she understood why. The entire parking lot next to the auto parts store was fenced: the narrow space was encircled with chain-link twelve feet high and topped with razor wire. Even if they were to scale the fence—and Carina wasn't sure Tanner could right now—they would never get past the razor wire: their enhanced abilities were no match for the deadly pointed barbs that would slice through their skin as easily as anyone else's.

Carina pushed Tanner behind a pair of Dumpsters as another bullet zinged past, followed by a rapid eruption of gunfire. Both men were shooting, and from the earsplitting echo of bullets on metal, the automatic rifle was cutting holes through the Dumpsters' sides.

Someone in the neighborhood would hear, wouldn't they? Someone must be calling the cops even now, right? The police might not be able to help them get the antidote, but it wouldn't matter if they didn't survive the next few minutes.

"Tanner," Carina said desperately. He was bent over, his hands on his good knee, his face pale. "I'm going to run and try to distract them, okay? Stay here."

"Run *where?*"

Carina had no idea. Beyond the lot, parked against the brick wall of the strip mall, was a rusting panel van that looked like it had been abandoned; the side was creased and dented from a collision, and one of the tires was flat. It wasn't much of a haven, but it would keep her safe, if only for a few seconds, and more importantly, it might distract the gunmen from Tanner. Even if she managed to draw only one of them, she'd give him a few more seconds of safety.

She bolted around the lot, a string of bullets following at her heels. At the van, she squeezed into the narrow space between it and the brick wall. Trying the door, she found it was locked, but the window was partly open. She reached in, the top of the glass cutting cruelly under her arm, grabbed the handle, and yanked.

Carina jammed the door open as far as possible, squeezing inside the passenger seat and grunting as her ribs were compressed between the door and the body of the van. She pulled the door shut behind her and crawled into the back. The metal floor was cold and hard on her knees, and the interior smelled like cigarette smoke and burned coffee. She looked around frantically for a weapon of any kind, but all she found was an empty coffee cup that had rolled under one of the seats.

Something was pressing against her hip—and suddenly Carina remembered the dart gun. How could she have forgotten it? She jammed her hand in her pocket and pulled out the gun. It was small and black, barely bigger than a water pistol. She could see the cartridge fitted into the barrel, which was open on the sides. A greenish liquid filled the tiny tube. The gun was simple in design; there was only the trigger, and a small slide that she figured was the safety. She snapped it forward just as something struck the side of the van and it rocked with the impact.

Someone shot out the driver's side window. Much more efficient, Carina had to admit as she cowered behind the backseat, than wedging himself through the passenger door as she had. She watched a hand, muscular and thick, grope for the door handle and yank it open.

The huge bald man climbed into the driver's seat. He was too big to squeeze easily past the steering wheel, which must have frustrated him, because he let loose what sounded a lot like cussing in another language, spraying the floor of the van with bullets as he forced himself between the two front seats.

Carina knew she had only one chance. The minute he

saw her, she was dead. She blinked, and an image of her mother—she'd aged so much, in that one year she had been away—flitted through her head. There were faint lines around her eyes, and there was a softness to the skin along her jaw. Her mother had suffered, and Carina, who had always wished for affection and warmth from her distant mom, realized the love had been there all along. Madelyn had simply never known how to show on the outside what she felt on the inside.

And now she was dead. And the man in front of Carina was one of her killers.

The fury inside Carina was suddenly unrestrainable. She rose to her knees, a guttural, furious cry escaping her lips, and with two hands aimed the pistol directly at the man's round, oily face.

She wasn't much of a shot. The gun bucked in her hand, and the dart lodged in the man's throat. He dropped his gun, pressing his hands to his neck, making a sound like air whooshing out of an inner tube. His lips moved as though he was trying to talk, and his eyes went glassy. Foam bubbled from his lips. He began to sink to the floor, his knees going out from under him.

Carina didn't intend to stick around to see what happened next. She thought about trying to get his gun, but he had collapsed on top of it, his breath coming in shallow gasps. There was no way she could move a man of that size—and besides, who knew what he was capable of, even in his compromised state; he looked like he had enough power in a single hand to strangle her.

Carina yanked up the lock and slid the side door open a few inches, staying behind it and wincing as she anticipated a hail of bullets.

But there was nothing. Far in the distance, she could hear sirens. Across the parking lot were the Dumpsters, but no sign of the second gunman. Glass littered the ground next to the van, and she stepped down cautiously, her shoes crunching on the shards.

Crouching low, she ran to the Dumpsters, praying that the gunman wasn't waiting for her behind them. Because that would mean that Tanner ... *No.* She wouldn't consider that, not until she had to.

She reached the Dumpsters and rounded the side, nearly colliding with Tanner, illuminated by a harsh streetlight. He was squatting, supporting himself against the wall with the backpack he had somehow held on to through the chase, an unreadable expression on his face. Placing a hand on his cheek, she felt his strong pulse, his warmth beneath her fingers. He was alive.

"Are you all right?" she whispered hoarsely.

He covered her hand with his own, holding it close against him, and nodded. "Car ..."

He swallowed hard and turned with effort. Carina followed his gaze.

There, unmoving and crumpled between the Dumpsters and the wall, his chest covered with a seeping stain, was the second gunman.

Dead.

CHAPTER THIRTEEN

Saturday, 3:34 a.m.
02:25:41

She knew he was dead by the lack of focus in his eyes. The fact that Tanner was alive was further proof: the two Albanians had not been about to let Carina or Tanner survive if they could help it. But if she had been unsure he was dead, the long, jagged piece of metal jutting from the bearded man's chest would have convinced her: it was embedded deep in his heart, and the area surrounding it was saturated with the blood that was dripping from his shirt into a growing pool on the ground.

"Are you all right? Where's the other guy?" Tanner asked.

"I'm fine. He's unconscious, I think. I shot him with the dart gun. Whatever was in there, it put him out. I guess if they increased the dose—"

"—to accommodate for the virus, it probably was enough to take out a horse," Tanner finished the thought. "Thank God you're okay, Car."

But she wasn't, not at all. Her vision was starting to flicker at the edges, as if her brain was short-circuiting as it processed information from the optic nerves. Her hands were trembling, and the smallest sounds pounded in her head like hammers. Her scalp itched, and it was only the memory of the man on the video pulling out his own hair that kept her from scratching at it.

But she couldn't let the symptoms of the infection interfere with what she had to do. "How did you ... ?"

Tanner lifted his hand and slowly unclenched his fist. Inside was another piece of metal, shorter than the one that had killed the bearded man but just as jagged.

"Where did you get it?"

Tanner's other hand slid down the side of the Dumpster, coming to rest on a metal band that had apparently once served to lock down the lid; a padlock dangled from the end. He pushed the metal and it clanged against the side of the Dumpster, the sound echoing hollowly in the space between the buildings.

"You ... broke it?"

"Yes." His voice was wooden.

"You literally tore off that piece of metal?"

Only then did Carina notice that some of the blood on Tanner's hand was fresh. It wasn't all from the wound in his leg. She could make out a few abrasions and cuts on his palm; ripping the metal had sliced through his flesh. She gasped and reached out to touch him. The piece of metal clanged to the ground as he finally let go of it.

Taking his hand gently, she pushed back his fingers. "Ow," he said. "That's a little tender."

"How did that ... thing get in *him*, is what I want to know. I mean, he had a gun, right? And even you aren't as fast as a bullet ..."

"I, uh, threw it."

"You—"

Suddenly she understood. Sometimes, when Tanner was bored, he practiced throwing knives in the backyard. Dull ones—old steak knives from his mom's kitchen drawer—at a homemade paper target fixed to a tree with a pushpin. It drove his mother crazy, and every time she caught him doing it she gave him extra dish duty, which he did without complaint—but Tanner insisted that working on his throwing accuracy this way increased his distance with the discus.

As if to illustrate her thought, Tanner picked up the piece of metal lying on the ground and got to his feet. He gingerly flexed the foot of his injured leg and set his weight on it, testing. Then he whipped the metal piece across the parking lot, straight at the van door that Carina had left open. The metal lodged in the upholstered seat, buried halfway, and the van rocked from the impact.

"If I keep this up, I'll go to the state championships for sure," he said, attempting a smile.

But Carina knew every one of Tanner's smiles. There was the easygoing one he flashed whenever he ran into friends, the cocky one when he won a heat at a meet, the gentle one when he helped his two middle brothers with their homework, and her favorite, his unguarded, pure happy-to-see-her grin, the one he reserved just for her.

This smile was like none of these. It was transparent, a ghost of a smile pasted over much deeper emotions. Horror. Guilt. Self-recrimination.

Tanner had just killed a man. And it was tearing him apart.

"Oh ...," Carina breathed, feeling like her lungs were being crushed. Tears pooled in her eyes, and she longed to take him in her arms, to comfort him the way he had comforted her when her uncle died. She wanted to take his pain away, the way he had for her.

She wanted ... But no, that wasn't entirely right. She *longed* for him, but this was different from the longing that took over her senses whenever they touched. This was a longing to be his strength, to be his support. To join herself with him so that together, they would be more than they were apart. Together, they would be enough—for any challenge, great or small. And it was hard to imagine any challenge greater than coming to terms with taking a life.

What she was feeling was more than longing, though. It was love.

Love. Carina tested the word in her mind as she gently caressed Tanner's face. She loved him; she knew that now. But love was the emotion she had feared above all others, the most terrifying, because it had always been linked with loss. And now Tanner was covered with his own blood, wounded, in just as much danger as she was. His chances of survival were made even worse by the gunshot wound in his leg. Loving him was the last thing a sensible person would do.

"Carina, please, run now, while you can," he said, as if sensing her thoughts. "Leave me here."

"I'm staying. The cops will be here soon." The sirens were coming closer, only blocks away now. "We'll be safe with them."

Tanner took a breath, wiping his hand on his shorts. "No. We won't. Think about it, Car: we've been involved in a homicide. Possibly two, since I didn't see anyone come out of the van but you. By the time the cops process the scene, straighten out who did what, it'll be tomorrow. I mean, it's already tomorrow. We've got less than three hours left. And those hours are going to be spent at the police station. There's no way they'll believe us if we tell them what's really going on."

"They have to," Carina said. "At least enough to call Sheila—her boss—someone—"

"And what, Sheila will rush over with the antidote? Even if she just conveniently happens to have it at home, there's no way she'd incriminate herself in that way. And to requisition it from the lab, even if they rushed through the steps—come on, Car, it's got top government security, there's no way it's happening in time."

With a sinking heart, Carina realized Tanner was right. If the cops found them, they were as good as dead. Frantically she scanned the empty lot, the street beyond, the nearby houses. The parking lots and streets were lit by unforgiving streetlamps, the cold yellow light barely casting shadows behind parked cars and fire hydrants. There was nowhere to hide, not with Tanner injured. She wasn't even sure he could walk.

And then her eyes lit on the drainage pipe that went under the road where it crossed the creek. The opening was about three feet across, large enough for an adult to crawl into. They had to get there—even if she had to carry Tanner, the way he had carried her earlier. She probably could, given all the other new capabilities she possessed. But before she tried, Carina had to do something she very much did not want to do: she crawled across the asphalt to the body of their would-be killer and looked for his gun. There—it had fallen near where he was sprawled. She had to move his leg slightly to get to it, and she did so with her foot, suppressing a wave of nausea. The weapon felt heavy in her hands.

"I'd put this in my pocket but, well, I don't want to shoot myself," she said.

Tanner was already standing up, and he started to take the backpack off his shoulders. Action brought some of the life back to his eyes. "I'll carry it, I'll—"

"Here," she said, pushing the pack back in place. She unzipped the outer compartment and dropped in the gun. "Okay. Now I need you to let me help you walk," she said, slinging his arm over her shoulders.

"I'll slow you down, I can't—"

"We're not going far."

She walked as fast as she could, Tanner keeping up better than she had dared hope. In fact, by the time they reached the ditch, he was almost walking on his own. Maybe it was shock that had immobilized him earlier—or maybe the virus helped heal him.

"Hurry," she urged, waiting for him to crawl into the pipe before she followed. He had to stay low, the backpack scraping the top of the pipe. Inside, there was an inch or so of standing water and a layer of slick mud. It smelled of rot and urine: someone else, probably homeless, had been here. For a moment she was afraid there were vagrants already inside, taking shelter for the night, because something blocking the other end kept any light from entering. But as they crawled deeper, feeling their way into the darkness, she found that it was trash wedged against a tangle of branches and dead foliage; at some point during the rainy season, the water had been high enough to sweep garbage into the pipe, and it hadn't yet been cleared.

They waited as the sirens came closer and closer, wincing as several vehicles passed overhead, the noise deafening and the vibration terrifying. The cars careened into the lot across the street, and then there was shouting, demands for them to show themselves, orders to drop all weapons. Little did the cops know they were talking to one dead man, and another one who—Carina prayed—was unconscious.

"How are you feeling?" she asked Tanner, trying not to show her concern. She could barely make out his features in the light that seeped into the pipe's opening. They couldn't stay here. The longer they remained, the more people would arrive who would notice a pair of teenagers—both filthy, one covered with blood—at the edge of the crime scene. If they went now, they might be all right; the cops' attention was riveted by the body they must have discovered by now.

"I'm ..." Tanner flexed his hands, then prodded his leg experimentally, wincing slightly. "I mean, I wouldn't want to run a marathon, but I'm all right. The bleeding stopped a long time ago. I haven't cramped up either, not since the first few minutes. Do you think—I mean, maybe the virus does other things too? Something to cut down on the bleed-ing?"

"I don't know. I mean, it's clear the bullet didn't hit any major arteries, or you'd be dead. I'm pretty concerned about all the filth that's gotten into the wound, but there's nothing we can do about that now. Do you think you can make a run for it?"

"I'll die trying," Tanner said grimly, a turn of phrase Carina wished he hadn't used.

Carina maneuvered her body around toward the tunnel opening.

And found herself staring into the face of the bald assassin.

CHAPTER FOURTEEN

Saturday, 4:09 a.m.
01:50:15

"Stupid bitch," the man wheezed in heavily accented English as he attempted to propel himself by brute force farther into the pipe.

There was something very, very wrong with him. His facial features were distorted and swollen, with great blotches of red marring his cheeks. His mouth was a grotesque leer, his tiny eyes practically disappearing into the folds of his skin. His breathing came in tortured rasps. Even his hands were swollen like cartoon mittens.

And yet, one of those hands was managing to hang on to a wicked-looking curved knife. He was clearly suffering some sort of reaction to the dart. He could easily have been disoriented, perhaps in pain.

If that was the case, however, he'd recovered enough to

follow them here. He must have eluded the police by reaching the ditch on the far side of the road before they arrived, and crawling toward the pipe out of sight. As if to counter any doubts Carina had about his abilities, the man took a swipe at her. If he'd been a few inches farther into the pipe, he might have cut her throat.

He struggled on his hands and knees to come farther inside, blocking most of the light, jabbing with the knife. But he was so large, and his coordination was so compromised by whatever was wrong with him, that he was having trouble.

Still, there was no escape route and no way, even with her heightened abilities, that Carina was going to be able to fend off a man who weighed more than twice what she did, especially since most of it was muscle and she was trapped in a space only a few feet wide. A few more seconds and he would crawl close enough to reach her with the knife; all it would take was one well-placed cut and she'd be dead. Then he could kill Tanner at his leisure.

That image—the man dragging her bleeding corpse out of the pipe to get to Tanner, wounded and trapped, infuriated Carina. She braced herself as well as she could, ignoring the pain in her knees from being pressed against rocks at the bottom of the pipe, and raised her hands, ready to try to fend off his jabs. Behind her, Tanner was grunting with the effort of clearing the debris blocking their exit, but with no tools and his wounded hands, he was making little progress.

The man inched forward, his breath sounding more like the whine of a motor than a human, drool hanging in strings from his rubbery, enormous lips. He swung with the knife again, and this time the tip sliced Carina's forearm, leaving a thin trail of glistening red. It was little more than a scratch, but his next attempt could certainly connect much deeper.

"No," Carina hissed, gritting her teeth. *You will not kill me. You do not get to hurt us. You will not win.*

She grabbed for his left arm, the one wielding the knife, and managed to catch his wrist on the backswing as he prepared to lunge. He tried to shake her off, but Carina focused all of her strength—which she'd won the hard way, with thousands of hours at the gym and track practice, as well as with the artificial boost she received from the virus—into holding on. He clamped his other hand over hers, attempting to pry it away, but Carina grabbed that one as well. She was holding both of his wrists while he twisted and pulled, trying to wrench free. She held tighter, focusing on her breathing, her pulse, forcing herself to assume a calm she didn't feel. To save herself and Tanner, she had to be better than she'd ever been before.

Not for the first time since being infected, Carina had the sense of time slowing down, of being able to experience every fraction of a second as though it was moments long, aware of every sensory detail that would ordinarily rush past in a blur.

And in the space of time it took for her to breathe in and out once, her daily appreciations flashed through her mind. Three things for which she was grateful, even now.

"Seeing my mom again. Tanner. And *this*," she whispered, watching confusion pass through the man's cruel little eyes.

She bent his wrists back.

At first it felt like trying to bend back a bar of steel, like she would never be able to repel the force and weight. She could hold him off, but not forever; there was still a limit to the duration of the bursts of strength she was capable of. Muscle contractions were still governed by the laws of biology. The chemical and mitochondrial realities were such that she would eventually need to rest.

But she had at least a few more seconds. She could feel her face flushing, her veins standing out as she pushed harder. The man emitted a sound like a kicked dog—and then that sound turned into a shriek as she felt something give. A tremor traveled through each of his arms, ligaments snapped ... and then there were two audible cracks. Carina pitched forward, her forehead bumping against the man's drool-covered, screaming face.

With her hands, she had broken both of his arms.

She was still holding on to his wrists, frozen with shock, but they flopped uselessly, the bone fragments grinding. The knife had clattered to the bottom of the pipe. The man's screams had turned into one long braying sound of agony, and only Carina's fear that someone would hear him got her moving again. She let go of his wrists, her stomach twisting in revulsion at seeing them hanging down from his ruined arms. He tried to lift them to his face and succeeded only in clubbing himself with his forearm.

Carina reached back and grabbed at the pile of debris that Tanner had been creating with the muck he'd managed to pull from the blockage. She seized a handful of mud and twigs and pebbles and jammed it into the man's open mouth, pushing the entire handful in before he had a chance to bite her. His screams ended with a choking gasp as he inhaled some of the stuff.

"I'm through!" Tanner said. Weak light streamed through a hole in the debris. "I think there's room—here—"

Moving forward, he shinnied through the hole in the blockage. Carina followed close behind, trying to ignore the frantic choking and gasping of the injured man. Branches painfully scraped at her exposed skin, and her hips got stuck for a moment, but she was able to push past, and in seconds she and Tanner were out of the pipe.

Carina glanced over at the parking lot and saw that several more police cars had arrived, a virtual swarm of vehicles. Their headlights lit up the scene. Only the gathering crowd of onlookers, people in workout gear and pajamas and bathrobes, all straining to see past the makeshift barrier that the police had erected, temporarily shielded them from view.

They crouched as they ran, partially hidden by the lower elevation of the creek bed. After half a block, another road crossed the creek, and they ran up onto the street and across lawns, into an alley, using the cover of darkness. Tanner was limping, but Carina barely had to slow down for him to keep up. After another quarter mile, they finally slowed.

Tanner took her hand, pulling her behind a tall, unkempt hedge where they were shielded from the views of even the closest neighbors.

"I broke . . . I broke . . ." Carina's teeth were chattering so hard she couldn't get the words out. She had broken the man's *arms*, snapped them like they were toothpicks. She had no idea if such an injury could be fixed, if he would ever heal. Whatever had been in the dart might have finished him off anyway—his breathing was so poor that he could easily be suffocating even now.

She'd shot that dart. If he died, she had killed him.

"You had no choice," Tanner said, pulling her close to him. "If you hadn't done something to stop him, he would have killed you."

"But *why?* I don't understand. I mean, Sheila's trying to pick me up alive so I can give her what she thinks I have. These guys—whether they believe I have Walter's data or not—want me *dead*."

Tanner was silent for a moment, thinking. "Someone who doesn't want you talking? Trying to protect the lab? There's millions, probably billions, of dollars invested in this research, not to mention people's reputations. If you talk, the whole thing's going to be shut down, and investigated pretty heavily."

"But what about their accents, Tanner? Sheila said that the Albanians want the virus for themselves. For their own army or mafia or whatever. If they think I have it, then they'd want me alive, not dead."

"But what if they have another source for the data? Or *think* they do? If they believe Sheila already has Walter's passwords? Then you become a complication, right? If they think you have the means to shut it down before they can get it?"

Carina realized Tanner was right. If she truly had a way to access Walter's backup data, then she could destroy it just as easily as she could share it, either with the help of the Army Criminal Investigation Command or on her own. And if someone else was trying to reach the data, but hadn't yet ...

Because their source at the lab hadn't turned it over ...

Because she didn't actually *have* it ...

"Oh my God," Carina breathed. "Sheila is selling the data to the Albanians. She promised it to them, but hasn't given it to them yet. They think she's stalling because of the money or something, but really it's because she doesn't actually have it—she thinks she needs me for that. She infects me to force me to trade the information for the antidote, because that way she has a surefire window of less than two days to get her hands on Uncle Walter's data."

"But meanwhile, they must have been following Sheila and you for days. And when we ran, at the funeral, they made a big assumption—a wrong one."

"That I had access to the data—"

"—and you were going to expose her. They see you arguing with her. They see us take off, and her guys go after us. They think Sheila's desperate to stop you before you turn her in."

"Because they know that's when the project gets shut down and they won't have access to the virus. Okay, I get it. But Tanner—one thing I still don't understand—how did they *find* us?"

"Well, we know how Sheila's guys found Walter's

place—my phone. They couldn't take us there, so they followed us to BART. All the Albanians had to do was watch what the Calaveras security team did, knowing it would lead them to you."

Carina shivered, thinking of the two sets of trained killers following them. For a moment she despaired, realizing what an amateur she was, thinking she could go up against professionals.

"Why didn't they just take us back at Walter's apartment? When we came out? We couldn't have made it easier for them...."

"I bet they tried. Car, the way Walter's got it set up, there's no way they could have gotten in...."

"But wouldn't we have heard them?"

"No way. He's got that door reinforced, and I'm sure it triggered some sort of alarm, but whatever it was, either Walter disabled it or we missed it somehow. Anyway, once they figured out what they were dealing with, they probably figured it was better to follow us and see where we went, rather than take us right away. After all, we'd already proved to them that we weren't hard to keep tabs on."

"So we managed to ditch the Calaveras guys, but not the Albanians. With Sheila's guys out of the way, they didn't have to be so careful—and we led them straight to my mom," Carina said, disgusted. "I can't believe we made it so easy! If we hadn't managed to get out of there ..."

"They'd have the password generator."

"I can't believe I got you into all of this," Carina said, her voice breaking. "Do you realize how many times now I've almost gotten you killed?"

"Yeah, I'm keeping track. You owe me half a dozen Double-Doubles. At least."

His crooked grin nearly broke her heart. The Double-Double—his favorite cheeseburger—was a long-standing joke between them ever since she beat him in their first climbing race, and he paid off the bet with a trip to In-N-Out.

She knew he was trying to keep her mind off the fact that in less than two hours, her body was going to start to destroy itself. And it almost worked, especially when he leaned in and kissed her, gently at first, and then more passionately.

His lips on hers were warm and soft. No one would ever guess that under their skin, a deadly pathogen was replicating and spreading through their blood. Carina wished she could get lost in the embrace, let it take them the way it had the other night, when reason gave way to passion and all her careful monitoring gave way to . . . love.

But every second that ticked by took them closer to death.

And Carina wasn't giving up that easily—not on her life, and not on Tanner.

She pulled away after one last kiss, her hand cupping his face. She searched his eyes, wondering how he could remain so steadfastly behind her. She'd infected him. Led him into danger. Gotten him shot.

"We're going to get through this" was what she settled for, even though the words would never be adequate. She took a deep breath and forced herself to concentrate. "Tanner—what about the IP address on the ring? What if it could help us get the antidote? I mean, it's a long shot … but even if it just gets us closer to Walter's research, it would give us something to bargain with."

"Okay, but we're going to need a wireless connection to check into it. Look, there's a Denny's at the next intersection. They probably have Wi-Fi and they're open twenty-four hours—think you can make it?"

Carina looked at the restaurant at the end of the shabby, run-down block. She had less than two hours left before she started to die, and this was the last place she would have chosen to spend it. "Yes, but what about you? Can you keep going?"

Tanner crouched and ran his fingers lightly along the edges of the wound, where the blood had dried on his shorts, a red so deep it looked almost black. "Well, it's definitely stopped bleeding. It's strange. I can feel it, but it isn't exactly pain, you know? Well, you probably don't know. It's got to be this virus."

He gingerly pushed his shorts up over his thigh. The wound—an area at the outer edge about three inches long— was jagged and messy, but already the worst of it seemed to be skimmed over with scar tissue.

"I mean, there's no damage to the bone or anything, and it's not like I can sterilize it now. Besides, I don't feel like it's going to slow me down. So my vote is, let's agree it's not even there, okay?"

"Tanner …"

"Car." He let the fabric fall back over the gash. "Look. We have to focus on now. Later, when we're … when things have calmed down, we'll worry about it. A little Neosporin and a couple Band-Aids, right?"

Carina doubted that topical first aid would do the trick, especially if an infection set in, which was likely, considering that the tissues had been in contact with filth and stagnant water. But she only nodded and forced a smile of her own. "Okay, then why are we still talking? Time is money."

She started running down the street, knowing Tanner would follow right behind her, hoping that the wind on her face would dry her tears before he had a chance to see them.

CHAPTER FIFTEEN

Saturday, 4:40 a.m.
01:19:33

It was a long city block to the Denny's, which sat on a busy street lined with liquor stores and nail salons and run-down apartment buildings. There were a few cars in the parking lot, a couple of people visible in booths behind the windows. Carina ran steadily, her feet hitting the pavement in rhythmic strides that didn't come close to winding her. Tanner kept up easily, and she could hear his breathing, steady and slow. If his leg was bothering him, it didn't show; the limp had also disappeared completely.

They slowed to a walk when they reached the sidewalk in front of the restaurant. Inside, they slid into an empty booth.

"Listen, I just had one other idea," she said.

"Name it."

"Well, it's just—you know that security guy, Baxter? He's always been good to me. And you saw how he was with Sheila—it's not like they're all that close. I was thinking, maybe he would help us? Maybe he'd let us into her office. She's got to have antidote stored there." *And we're running out of time,* she didn't add.

But she didn't have to. Tanner frowned, his eyebrows knitting together. It was taking a hell of a chance, but they didn't have a lot of options left.

"You know how to reach him?"

"Yes, Mom made me learn his cell number a long time ago, the first time I ever came to a company event."

Tanner dug the phone out of the backpack and handed it over. Carina dialed. It had only begun to ring when it was picked up.

"Baxter."

"Hey, Baxter . . . this is Carina."

"Where are you?" His tone was clipped, urgent; Carina reminded herself that he was trained for situations like this.

"Look, um, I have to ask you a favor. I mean a really, really big favor."

"Anything."

"And Sheila can't know, okay? I mean, she really can't—"

"My loyalty was to your uncle. And to your mother."

The relief that coursed through Carina was almost overwhelming. "Look, we need to get into Sheila's office. We don't have much time. Can you help us?"

"Yes." He answered without hesitation. "I have master clearance."

"Can you pick us up? I mean, alone? We're in South San Francisco."

"I can be there in a half hour. What's your location?"

Tanner had been leaning in close enough to hear both sides of the conversation. Before she could answer, he squeezed her hand and pointed across the street at a run-down little park, whispering in her ear, "Don't say we're at Denny's."

"We'll wait for you in a park," she told Baxter. She gave him the cross streets and hung up, praying that she wasn't making the biggest mistake of her life.

"We're cutting this really close," she said. "Half an hour for him to get here, then at least an hour to the lab . . ."

"Don't think about that. He might be here sooner. Let's work on our plan B. Give me the address and I'll get started."

She took the pen Tanner handed her and quickly did the hex conversion on the back of her place mat, then slid it across the table. "Do you mind if I go try to clean up a little?"

"No problem, I was thinking the same thing. You go first, I'll order."

Carina walked quickly through the restaurant, trying not to draw attention, but no one even glanced at her disheveled appearance. Luckily, there was no one in the bathroom. Carina soaked a stack of paper towels and went to work. First she dabbed away all the dirt on her skin; her ankles and calves had been liberally streaked with mud. She scrubbed her hands until her nails were as clean as she could get them, then went to work on her clothes. After trying to get the dirt off with towels, she soon decided it was a lost cause. Instead she stripped and ran water over the clothes, and turned her attention to her hair. Her hat had come off at some point in their escape, and her hair was tangled and dirty. Without a comb, she had to settle for using her fingers, but at least she was able to get out all the small twigs and leaves, and with a little water she was able to smooth it into almost-intentional-looking waves.

She only dared run the dryer through three cycles, so the clothes were still wet when she put them back on and she winced with the clammy chill. But at least they—and she—were a bit cleaner.

Tanner was sitting in a booth as far away as possible from the other customers, one with a view of the park so they could see Baxter when he arrived—and make sure he was alone. He had also managed to clean himself up, wiping most of the blood off so he looked relatively normal. He was hard at work on the laptop, two steaming cups on the table next to it—along with two plates loaded with toast, eggs, and bacon. Carina didn't realize how hungry she was until her stomach growled in anticipation. She grabbed a fork and took a huge bite.

It was crazy. If she didn't get the antidote soon, she was dead, but she wolfed down her food like she was preparing for a multiday siege.

"Pay dirt," Tanner muttered, not looking up as his fingers flew over the keys, taking breaks only to eat. "That IP address? Server farm in Transnistria."

"Trans ... what?" Carina asked, taking a sip of coffee. It tasted like heaven.

"Transnistria. Breakaway territory from Moldova. Post–Soviet conflict zone, no one can touch it in any official capacity ... got all kinds of illicit shit going on...."

"Okay, let's file that under more than I need to know."

"Gotta admire Walter, though."

"I do. Believe me. So what's on there?"

Tanner raised his eyebrows and spun the laptop toward her. He grabbed a piece of toast and wolfed down half of it in two bites as Carina scanned the screen.

"This means nothing to me," she said, scrolling through dozens of directories and hundreds of files with cryptic names and extensions she'd never seen before.

"It's the real thing, Car, as far as I can tell."

"Okay," Carina said, turning the computer back toward Tanner. "And you got there with that clicker thing?"

"Yeah, got in first try. Pretty amazing."

"Where is it now—did you put it back in your sock?"

"Yeah...." He tapped his ankle, where the token generator bulged from the small pocket, and then his voice trailed off as he started tapping the keys again. Carina recognized the look of glazed concentration, and she slowly pushed the laptop lid closed on his fingers.

"Hey!" he protested, but he was smiling, and he held up his hands in defeat. "Fine, fine, but I'd sure love to see inside his process—"

"Maybe later. For now, we have places to go. Things to see. Eat up, you're going to need the energy."

Tanner was already moving on to the bacon. "What's next?" he added through a mouthful.

"Well, considering that we're"—*mere moments from death,* she had been about to say, but she didn't have the heart.

Tanner swallowed and took a sip of coffee, his expression instantly subdued. "Yeah," he said quietly. "We really are out of options, aren't we?"

"I don't know what else to do. The Albanians—who knows if there's more of them, right? And since we don't know how they found us the first time, we have to assume they'll be able to find us again. They probably have reinforcements on their way."

"Okay. . . . Well, you want to call her from here?"

Carina was silent for a moment. A thought had been nagging at her for a while, one she had been afraid to confront.

If they called Sheila, she would probably demand proof that they had Walter's data before giving them the antidote. She might even refuse to trade until the information was in her hands.

And if that happened, she was sure to sell it. The virus and antidote would be bound together using Walter's research and turned into a product that could be in foreign hands in no time, and an army halfway across the world would soon be arming its soldiers with powers that would enable them to crush anyone they wanted to in hand-to-hand combat. Their advantage could conceivably tip the balance of power in unstable nations; if they in turn sold it to others, the nature of war itself could be affected.

But the only other option was to destroy the password

generator and then take their own lives. If she called the major, she had enough to get the lab shut down and Sheila arrested. Work on the virus would halt, and its leakage into the world could be prevented. If they were lucky, no one would ever again die from exposure to the virus.

She and Tanner could be the last.

Carina shut her eyes, remembering the last night she saw Walter, how distracted he'd been. How he'd hesitated before going up to his room, as though there was something he wanted to say.

And her mother, throwing her arms around Carina tonight. The year she'd spent in agony, knowing her daughter thought she was dead. The awkward "I love you" that had been there all along, buried so deeply that it took all this suffering to finally bring it out.

Walter and her mother, both of them gone. Both dead. Without them, what did Carina have to live for? She might as well end her own life. It wouldn't have to be the horrible, painful decline from the virus. She could step in front of a train, fall from a tall building. There were dozens of ways to die, even for a body infected with the virus. Carina wasn't sure she believed in any kind of afterlife, but if there was one, she would be sharing it with the only people who had ever loved her.

Carina opened her eyes and found Tanner watching her, his expression knowing and infinitely sad. Because he knew her so well.

"Carina. No."

"What do you mean, no? How can you know what I'm thinking?"

He shook his head and sighed. "I don't know. Because I'm in love with you and think of you all day long? Because the other night made me feel even closer to you, when I already felt like we're the same person half the time?"

Love . . . love. Carina heard the other words he spoke, but her heart got stuck on that one and it reverberated inside her, taking over everything else.

So it wasn't an isolated thing. Tanner was going to keep using the L-word, at least every time they were in life-or-death situations, and Carina found that she didn't exactly want him to stop.

In fact, right now, she sort of needed him to keep doing it.

"We're not doing . . . that," Tanner continued, before she could say anything. "We're not going out without a fight. We've been fighting hard. I feel weird as shit. I know it's going to get worse as we get closer to the end, but there's a part of me, a very big part, that hasn't even begun to kick ass yet."

Carina couldn't help it—a smile tugged at the corners of her mouth, and a little shiver ran along her spine like a trill played on a flute.

Tanner stiffened, looking out the window. "Baxter came through," he said softly, whistling under his breath.

Sure enough, in front of the park across the street, a familiar dark sedan idled. While they watched, Baxter got out of the car and scanned the interior of the park.

Tanner put some bills on the table, loaded the laptop into the backpack, put it on, and they headed for the exit.

"Tanner . . ."

"Hmm?"

She took a deep breath. "If—*when*—we get out of this, remind me that I have something to tell you."

"You can't tell me now?" Tanner said, holding the door open for her. Outside, dawn was breaking, the sky streaked with pink and gold. Behind Carina, a woman carrying a purse and a coffee cup smiled gratefully as Tanner held the door for her too.

Carina might have told him—what he'd come to mean to her, how close to giving up she'd come. That she needed him and couldn't imagine life without him.

But as she opened her mouth to speak, the woman who had been behind her stepped in front of them, and her head exploded.

CHAPTER SIXTEEN

Saturday, 5:12 a.m.
00:47:14

The woman fell facedown on the asphalt, twitching spas-
modically. Screams erupted inside the restaurant. Only the
fact that they were blocked by the open door had protected
Carina and Tanner from the blood and gore that splattered
the ground. Hovering in the air a few yards away was what
looked like a huge black insect with four wings protrud-
ing from its body, each with whirring antennae, holding it
aloft. As Carina watched in horror, the flaps folded in with
a mechanical whir, like an origami box made by invisible
hands. The thing darted left, hovering for a second, then
sped away, flying up and over the roof of the building, disappearing into the lightening sky.

"Drone!" Tanner yelled, grabbing her arm. She didn't
need to be told that it was time to go, and she ran alongside

him in a frantic exercise that was becoming all too familiar: putting the latest danger behind them and praying they weren't headed into another. They raced across the parking lot, over a grassy berm in front of an office building next to the strip mall.

"Why'd it take off?" Carina asked as they leapt over a winding stone path, their movements in tandem, a stride that would have had them both placing in any long-jump event from the last track season. "I mean, it got the wrong target, right?"

She winced as she said the word. It hadn't been a *target*—it had been a *woman*, a living, breathing human being.

"Don't know, but I'm guessing it's because it only had the capacity to fire one explosive. Once it delivered the payload, it's probably programmed to return to its base."

"So it's like a little flying robot?"

"Yeah. And it probably isn't the only one."

Terror seized Carina's nerves, turning them to ice. She stopped under the overhang at the entrance, scanning the few people outside. A custodian smoked next to his supply cart. A man with a briefcase opened the door with a key.

Frantically, she looked around, and when she saw it—a tiny dot still so high in the sky it looked like nothing more threatening than a bumblebee—she gasped.

"We have to get inside that building!" she said, pulling at Tanner's hand.

"Car, wait—it's going to follow us. One of us must be wearing a tracking device."

"*What?* How?"

"I don't know, but—"

Carina didn't hear the rest because she was backing away in horror, putting distance between her and Tanner and the other people gathered near the building. There was no sign of Baxter; glancing down the street, she didn't even see his car.

If there really was a tracking device, it would be on her, because she was the one they wanted dead. And there was no way she was risking another innocent person's life. She didn't know much about drone technology, but it must not have been perfected yet, since the other one had hit the wrong target.

So she would just draw it away from everyone else and then . . . do something. Her mind was blank, but she still had a few seconds to come up with a plan.

Except the thing was coming closer, bearing down on them at what looked like twenty-five or thirty miles an hour.

And it was headed for Tanner.

"Watch out!" Carina screamed. Tanner hadn't seen it yet; he was crouched in a ready stance, looking all around. The drone was twenty feet away and closing in fast, and Carina did the only thing she could think of.

She raced toward it, raising her fist in the air. When she got between the drone and Tanner, it was only a few feet away, and she was close enough to see that the flaps on top had opened and a metal structure with a blinking red light had risen from its center.

The light was pointed straight at Tanner.

Carina leapt into the air, pushing off with her calves from

the balls of her feet, throwing her head back and propelling herself harder than she ever had. As her momentum carried her forward, she swung her fist, and in the slow-motion shutter click of time that she had come to recognize as the virus's way of handling sudden bursts of exertion, she saw it make contact with the drone, striking the open flaps. It careened over and over, away from them, knocked from its trajectory but not from its programmed task of firing a kill shot, because a split second later there was a crashing sound and a chunk of the overhang fell to the ground. The drone wobbled, making a sound like a shorted fuse, and fell jerkily to earth, its flaps fluttering uselessly. Carina ran to it: up close, it looked like a child's toy, well under a foot long, its firing mechanism broken as though an overly energetic eight-year-old had played with it too zealously.

Tanner reached her side in seconds. "I don't see any more," he said, helping her up. "But that doesn't mean they aren't there."

The two men near the entrance were staring at the piece of the overhang that had fallen. The man with the cart started backing toward the side of the building, then turned and took off running. None of them seemed to notice Carina and Tanner or realize they had been the targets of the drone. Off in the distance they heard sirens for the second time that day, screaming toward the poor woman lying dead in front of the Denny's.

They ran.

《◆》

The park no longer offered the safety they needed, and Carina and Tanner hurtled down the street looking for shelter. As they passed shops, a bank, early-morning joggers, Carina's mind raced just as frantically to figure out where they could go to be safe, without endangering others. A bunker would have been nice—some steel-walled, underground barrack where they could wait out the attack.

But the Albanians seemed determined enough to keep trying new tactics until they found one that worked. What would be next—robots armed with flamethrowers? An armored tank?

Second best would be an empty, windowless building. If nothing else, they could buy some time to figure out what to do next. But there were innocent people around: delivering newspapers, opening bakeries and coffee shops, walking to the bus stop. Carina thought of taking shelter in a car, but the risk was too great that the vehicle's owner might come out and put himself in the line of fire by accident, even if they could find one that was unlocked.

But suddenly, up ahead, she saw a man unloading crates of soda from a truck parked outside a 7-Eleven. He positioned a final crate on a wheeled dolly and began pushing it toward the entrance.

"There!" Carina yelled, and Tanner nodded, veering off toward the truck.

Tanner kicked the ramp leading from the truck so hard that the hinges broke and it clattered to the street. He slammed the doors shut, creating an even louder commotion, and Carina knew they had very little time.

She raced around to the driver's side, already hearing the driver screaming at her from the sidewalk, praying that the truck wouldn't have a manual transmission. She pulled herself up and into the driver's seat and let out a sob of relief upon seeing the keys dangling from the dashboard. Tanner was pulling himself into his own seat when she started the truck. She veered off into the street, one back wheel going over the curb and causing the truck to shudder and bounce. Horns blared as a pickup swerved to make room for her. She was sure they would draw the attention of any cops around; she hoped they were all responding to the Denny's incident and the gory scene that awaited them.

"Down that side road!" Tanner yelled, pointing at the mall in the next block.

Carina swerved into the nearly empty parking lot. Along the side of the anchor store, a service lane led around to the back. She turned down it, glancing in her rearview mirror to make sure no one was following. The owner of the truck was surely calling it in right now, and as Carina pulled around behind the building she breathed a sigh of relief: with any luck they could stay hidden here for a little while.

She pulled up next to the graffiti-covered metal doors behind a kitchen-supply store and turned the engine off. For a moment she just sat with her hands glued to the wheel, breathing hard, not from exertion but from anxiety.

"Way to go, Dale Earnhardt," Tanner said. "Didn't know you had it in you."

"Me either."

Carina turned to face him as he unbuckled his seat belt,

that trademark crooked grin looking only a little worse for wear.

"We lost Baxter somehow," Carina said. Tanner pulled off the backpack and opened the top. Rummaging around inside, he handed her the disposable cell phone.

"Carina," Tanner said softly. "It's too late for him to help."

Tears filled her eyes as she realized it was true. They were out of time. There was no way they could get to the lab in the next half hour, no matter how fast Baxter drove; their only hope was Sheila. Any noble fantasies Carina had had of destroying the ring and the password generator and then taking their own lives were forgotten. She couldn't sacrifice Tanner, even if it meant the possibility of saving others.

And she knew he felt the same way.

She dialed Sheila's number. The day she'd memorized it—standing in Sheila's kitchen, trying to come to terms with the fact that this was going to be her new home, now that she was completely alone—seemed like it had been a century ago.

There was a click as the phone was picked up.

"Took you long enough," Sheila said, not bothering with hello. "You're flirting with your own death, you know that, right? But then, I guess I shouldn't expect anything less. After all, you are your mother's daughter."

CHAPTER SEVENTEEN

Saturday, 5:33 a.m.
00:26:53

"She knows about my mom," Carina said after she hung up, her throat dry.

"That she's dead?"

"No. That she faked her own death. She's known all along, Tanner. She said I'm my mother's daughter."

"That doesn't mean anything, necessarily," Tanner said as he took the phone back from Carina, who was gripping it so tightly he had to gently pry her fingers off. "Maybe she just found out. If her people somehow tracked us to your mom—"

"But how? We lost the security guys in the BART station. If one of us does have a tracker somehow, it's the Albanians who are following the signal, not Sheila."

"Sheila could have more guys after us. The entire security team, for all we know. But I guess it doesn't matter now."

Sheila had told Carina to sit tight, that she'd be there as fast as she could, fifteen minutes tops.

"And she's bringing the antidote?"

"Yes, she promised."

"Okay, well, we still need to worry about the tracker. We could be sending out a signal. And even if they've run out of drones, or drone cannons or whatever those things were, they could already be on their way to kill us the old-fashioned way."

The fact that she and Tanner had put down two of their guys wasn't going to deter them for long, Carina guessed. She shuddered to think that more armed, ruthless operatives could be on their way to the mall right now.

"It has to be me," Tanner said. "The drone came after me."

"So it had to be the guy with the beard who put it on you, right? Tanner, think about what happened back at the Dumpster—did he get close enough to you to attach something?"

"I—after he went down. I went over to . . . to make sure." Tanner swallowed. "He wasn't quite dead. He lunged at me. I mean, kind of threw himself at me—I got out of the way fast. I banged into the wall, hit my knee on the ground, just trying to get away from him. It felt like he just wanted to pound me, and I'm not sure I would have noticed him putting something on me."

"But he could have—"

"Yeah." Tanner pulled his shirt up and over his head, then began stripping off his shorts.

Carina checked every inch of the blood- and dirt-crusted

cotton, finding nothing other than a few bits of twigs that had snagged on the fabric. She checked the shorts Tanner handed her too; it took longer because she had to go through every pocket, along every seam. When she was finished, Tanner got dressed again in the filthy clothes.

"Damn!" he exclaimed as he pulled the shirt back on. He was feeling along his back, a few inches behind his left armpit. "I can't see, Car, but there's something here."

Carina bent close, her face only inches from his skin. There was something. . . . At first she thought it was a mole, but soon saw it was a metal bead, buried in his flesh.

"When he attacked me," Tanner said. "I can't believe I forgot that. It must have been a backup—like, if they lost their weapon they were still instructed to get the tracker on us. Wow, can you imagine the discipline it would take? If you knew you were finished, you were basically dead, but you still kept your wits about you enough to help the next guy finish the job?"

Carina didn't want to think about it. "The tracker was supposed to be for me," she said. "You were just in the way."

"You were over in the van with the other guy. I guess he figured it was better than nothing. Can you get it out?"

"Yeah, I'll just pull . . ."

She closed her thumbnail and fingernail around the small bead and tugged. To her surprise, it didn't move.

"Ow!" Tanner exclaimed. "I mean, sorry, don't mind me, just keep pulling. But shit, that hurt."

Carina squinted and looked closer. She'd thought the device was attached with a simple needle, like the dart containing the poison, but when she tugged at it, the skin didn't give way. It must have exploded on impact, embedding itself with multiple barbs, much like a fishhook.

"You sure you want me to do this?" Carina asked doubtfully. Given the technology that the Albanians had proved capable of, she was afraid to find out what would happen.

"You have to," Tanner said, gritting his teeth.

So Carina anchored her fingers around the bit of metal, took a deep breath, and pulled with all her might.

The sound Tanner made was like that of a wounded bear, half growl and half cry. What came out in Carina's hand was unbelievable: the bead was connected to half a dozen long, narrow blades jutting outward from the center; these had lanced under the skin and through Tanner's tissues on impact, anchoring the device firmly; but when they were torn free they left behind pulped, bloody flesh.

Carina sat frozen, staring at the spiderlike assemblage of metal and plastic with an electronic chip at its core. It was easily four inches across, and it had left a wound at least that large on Tanner's back.

"God, I hope I don't faint," Tanner said weakly, clamping his hand over the mess, blood streaming through his fingers. "Get that thing out of here, please, or I will have given up the left side of my body for no good reason."

Carina snapped out of her shock. "Be right back," she promised. Then she was out of the truck and running, fast, around the side of the mall. She passed a few employees heading toward the entrance, deliverymen and maintenance workers.

She didn't know how much time she had. How long had it been since she'd called Sheila—five minutes? Ten? She ran through the parking lot, threading her way between cars, the thing in her hand still warm from Tanner's body.

Up ahead, an area of the parking lot was roped off where they were repairing the median. The earthmoving equipment sat idle and unoccupied; the crew probably wouldn't return until Monday. Perfect. When she got within several car lengths from the edge, she threw the tracker as hard as she could, watching it bounce off the edge of the bulldozer's giant tire before coming to rest in a mound of dirt.

Thoughts of Tanner alone and bleeding made Carina turn and run back. She rounded the corner of the mall again, mindful of people staring at her, hoping they wouldn't report her to mall security.

There—the truck was where she had left it. She ran for the door and jerked it open, pulling herself up into the driver's seat and slamming the door behind her.

Tanner was gone.

The backpack was abandoned on the floor. The empty passenger seat was smeared with blood. On the door handle, a bloody handprint.

"Oh God, Tanner, oh no!" Carina wailed.

Behind her, the driver's-side door was flung open. Carina twisted around in her seat, staring down at Sheila.

The woman gave her a smile that made up in irritation and impatience what it lacked in warmth.

"Looking for your boyfriend?"

"What have you done with him?"

Sheila stepped nimbly out of the way as Carina lunged. Behind her, Baxter waited, leaning back against his long, sleek sedan. It was idling in the shadow of the building, which was how Carina had missed it as she'd run from the truck.

"Baxter...," she breathed in disbelief. Had he turned them in? Or was he only here because Sheila had summoned him? His face was unreadable behind the mirrored sunglasses.

"Your boyfriend's fine, other than that hole in his back that he refuses to explain," Sheila said wearily. "Also, he insists that you went out to get a bagel, but you don't seem to have one.... Did they run out?"

Carina took a deep breath to keep herself from punching Sheila in the face. "I have to warn you, Sheila, I do not have a lot of impulse control at the moment," she snarled. "See, there's this virus that is doing all kinds of crap to me, and I don't think I can be held responsible for what I do to you."

Sheila rolled her eyes. "Oh, for heaven's sake, Carina, calm down. I am getting a little tired of your whole teenage angst thing. In these brief few days, you've made me wish I'd never agreed to be your guardian."

"Not as much as Walter, I bet."

A look passed through Sheila's eyes that surprised Carina: hurt. Deep, genuine hurt. But she didn't let her smile slip. "No, I suppose not. Here's what's funny, though. You've been running around all night looking for the antidote, I take it? Is that right?"

"More or less," Carina said begrudgingly.

"Well, what on earth do you think was in that dart gun you took off the guard in the BART station?"

Carina's mouth dropped open. "What are you talking about?"

"The darts that my men were trying to shoot you with. What did you think they were doing?"

"Uh ... trying to knock me out, obviously, so they could bring me back to you."

"Half right. The plan was to bring you in safely while the virus was eradicated from your system. I did want you back here, but only so I could keep you safe. Which, obviously, you can't even begin to handle on your own."

"If it really wasn't you who infected me—or at least ordered it done—how would you even know it had happened?"

"I received an anonymous tip," Sheila said. "Or more precisely, a threat. The morning of the funeral. I've had people trying to trace it around the clock."

"I don't believe you," Carina snapped. "I shot a guy with whatever was in that gun. He ... he ..." The image of his face, swollen and grotesque, came back to her.

Sheila rolled her eyes. "The antidote is an incredibly powerful drug, and it's a shock to the system if a person isn't infected. Don't worry, he'll recover fully."

Other than the two ruined arms, Carina thought. Her confusion was growing; the earth seemed to be shifting under her. Was it possible that Sheila was telling the truth?

"Look, Carina, I've made a lot of mistakes in my life," Sheila said. "I admit there were a lot of things I didn't handle well. Believe me—I'd change things if I could. But please, just take a look at this. I'm going to move slow here...."

She backed up to the car while Baxter watched impassively.

Sheila opened the door and there, inside, was Tanner, looking a lot better than he had a few minutes ago. Meacham was sitting next to him, taping a bandage over the wound in his back. Tanner looked up at Carina, an apology in his eyes.

"Show her," Sheila said, and Meacham held up a black dart gun identical to the one Carina had left on the floor of the van after shooting the Albanian with it. Horrified, Carina remembered the foam that had spewed from his mouth when she shot him—but Tanner showed no signs of an adverse reaction. "Your boyfriend's well on his way to recovery now," Sheila added, as if reading her mind. "Give that antidote another hour and he'll be feeling a lot more like himself."

"How do I know you didn't poison him?" she demanded.

"Oh, please. Look at him. You're going to have to trust me here, Carina. I'm trying to help you. Yes, it's true that someone inside the organization is working with the Albanians. Your mother was the first one to figure out that there was a leak, and I'll admit, when she disappeared I got scared. When Walter started talking about the antidote a few months ago I begged him to stay quiet, but he wanted to get the Army Criminal Investigation Command involved. I..." To Carina's astonishment, Sheila's voice broke. "I was afraid something terrible would happen. And I was right. I kept telling Walter to keep things quiet, to stop stirring things up. We fought about it. The whole time I just … I've never been good at … Well, it doesn't matter now."

Her face was a twisted mask of anguish and fury, and Carina slowly realized that she had had Sheila all wrong.

Sheila wanted something desperately, enough to compromise her job. But it wasn't money.

It was Walter.

Sheila had been in love with Walter, but she'd never been able to express it, and he'd mistaken her attempts to dissuade him from his work for evasiveness. He'd suspected her of being the leak, the one who'd reached out to the foreign buyers, when all along she'd been trying to keep him safe.

"Then who is it?" Carina demanded. "Who's really working with the Albanians?"

"Look, let's get you the antidote and then we'll talk," Sheila said.

"Not until you tell me."

More eye rolling. "Carina, honey, if you and I are going to live together, you are going to *have* to work on this trust thing. I just fixed up your boyfriend. I spent my Friday evening racing around town trying to find you. Don't you think you could cut me a little slack? The short answer is that we don't know. I've been in touch with Major Wynnside and I'm meeting with him next week. There's going to be a covert investigation, to try to flush out the guilty parties without tipping them off that we're looking. There's more to it, but—"

"Not a whole lot more, really," Baxter said.

Sheila looked at him in surprise. Carina did too.

"What are you talking about?" Sheila demanded.

"I said there's not much more to it. Someone on the inside got tired of working for peanuts, figured there was a lot of money to be made here, and did a little simple cold-calling, trying to drum up business."

He reached inside his coat, and when his hand came out it was holding a gun, pointed at Sheila.

"You never asked me what I did before I came to Calaveras," he said mildly.

"What are you ..." Sheila looked aghast. Behind her, Tanner got out of the car, his expression wary, and started circling around toward Carina. Meacham clambered out after him and stood looking from one person to the next, clearly confused.

"If you'd ever bothered to ask, I would have told you that I was a business major in college. I was going to take over the family business. Little chain of banks in Wisconsin. My grandfather started it." He laughed bitterly. "Of course, you may have heard that the banking industry ran into a little trouble back a few years ago. Whoops. Dad narrowly missed going to jail, and we lost the banks. I had to take the first job I could get."

"But that's not—"

"And then once I'd been on the job awhile, I figured out that I could make easier money selling classified research than low-interest checking accounts. Besides, you can't think I *like* working for you," he demanded, anger edging his words. "You're a real pain in the ass, Sheila."

"I'll have your job for this," Sheila said angrily. "You're never going to—"

He shot her.

A neat little hole appeared in the center of her forehead and she stumbled backward, her eyes wide, staring in surprise. Before Carina could scream, Baxter pivoted slightly and shot Meacham, who fell in a heap like a bag of rags.

Then he turned the gun on Tanner.

CHAPTER EIGHTEEN

Saturday, 6:00 a.m.
00:00:00

"No, no, don't!" Carina screamed, pushing herself in front of Tanner.

"Why shouldn't I?" Baxter asked, caressing her face with the barrel of the gun. The metal was cold on her skin and she flinched. "I have everything I need right here, with you."

Carina swallowed. "I won't give you anything if you hurt him."

"Really?" Baxter raised his eyebrow. "Very noble, but how are you going to feel when you start twitching and pulling out your own hair?"

"It was you," Carina said, a chill going through her. "You infected me. Where did you do it? The salon?"

Baxter chuckled. "No, though that would have been a nice idea, but my *boss* wasn't one to give me a lot of information about her personal calendar. Though she felt comfortable yanking me around any hour of the day. Treated me like her personal slave, most of the time. But no, I had to figure out that little detail without her help. It wasn't all that hard. . . . Sheila was kidding herself if she thought that so-called security system of hers was worth a damn."

"You broke into her apartment?"

"You make it sound like a *bad* thing." Baxter showed his perfect white teeth in an all-American grin. "I just paid a visit over my lunch hour, left you a little something on your toothbrush. Very nice bathroom, by the way. Some of the girls I date ought to learn from your example, clean and neat. Most of them leave their crap everywhere, makeup, hair on the floor. . . . Can't stand that."

Carina wasn't listening. She was remembering—getting ready for her date with Tanner. Putting on makeup. Picking out an outfit.

Brushing her teeth.

It had been after seven o'clock. Not six o'clock, as she'd assumed, which meant that she still had a little time. She wasn't dead just yet. The relief that flooded through her lasted only a second, though.

"Why didn't you just take me then?" she demanded furiously. "If you figured out how to get in, you could have kidnapped me when I got back from the salon."

"Yeah, but I needed a little more time to make sure no one ended up blaming me. My plan was brilliant, I have to say. The morning of your uncle's funeral, after he was safely in the ground, Sheila received an anonymous text saying that you'd been infected. I couldn't be sure which of you Walter would have trusted. I needed you both. You were my insurance, because I knew Sheila would do anything to save you."

"But if she thought I was infected, why wouldn't she just give me the antidote?"

"That's exactly what she'd do. Only, she wouldn't have brought it to the memorial service. She'd have to go back to her house or the lab for it. And who do you think she would have brought along on such a critical mission?"

Carina's head spun at his words. The whole time, she'd thought Sheila was trying to use her, that she didn't care about her. That Sheila would allow her to die, if necessary.

But she—and Walter—had been wrong about her.

"That's right," Baxter said, nodding smugly. "Her crack security team. Me and that dumbass Meacham. You know how long I've put up with that clown? Oh well, looks like I'll be working solo now." He chuckled.

"So you were going to wait until we were all in the car after the service—"

"And then we wouldn't have gone back to her place at all. I had a nice little setup out near Red Rock Canyon State Park. Little cabin up there, been in Meacham's family forever. The guy couldn't stop talking about it; he used to invite me up there to camp. Ha. I would have put him down first, tossed him in the lake. He could have spent an eternity on his family land.

"And then you and I and Sheila would have waited in the cabin. I took precautions—there's supplies up there to last a week. Not that I figured it would take more than a few hours for you and Sheila to break down, once she remembered what your future held. You and she'd be *begging* to do the trade."

"Except for one thing—we didn't have it."

"I know that now." More chuckling. "I swear, it's like I've got a little guardian angel sitting on my shoulder. If you and your boyfriend hadn't bolted, you never would have ended up at your uncle's hidey-hole, or on his little treasure hunt."

"When you shot her at the BART station—" Tanner said angrily.

"Totally harmless. Mild sedative, I substituted it myself. I needed her unharmed, of course. You, I didn't give a shit about, a waste of bullets. I just didn't factor in the virus, which attacks the compounds in the sedative. Yeah, don't look so surprised. I minored in biology."

"And then you tracked us using the phone?" Tanner demanded.

"Yeah, Boy Scout. That's what you get for playing out of your league. It was just bad luck that once you got on the train again, I picked the wrong station. Meacham and I had gone to Embarcadero, figuring you'd be heading back to the East Bay. And instead you went to Civic Center, where Sheila had sent the B team. You can bet that if I'd been there, things would have played out differently."

"And this whole time, Meacham never knew what you were up to?"

"Yeah. Poor dumbass. I think he lost the thread somewhere back at the memorial service, but he was a good soldier. Did what he was told. Listen, this is fun and all, but I'd like to get going, and I imagine you're in a bit of a hurry too. I'm assuming you've got everything I need now, right?"

"No," Tanner and Carina said at once.

"There wasn't anything in the locker," Tanner said.

"We still don't know where he stored his backups," Carina added. She knew neither of them was a credible liar, and Baxter merely raised an eyebrow.

"You'll forgive me for not taking your word for it. Go ahead and assume the position."

He pointed to the hood of the car, and Carina and Tanner put their hands on the warm metal while he patted them down. Carina squeezed her eyes shut at his touch, trying to quell the nausea that passed through her. When he started on Tanner, she watched from the corner of her eye, breathing a sigh of relief when he stopped short of Tanner's socks and shoes. Next he went through the backpack, checking every pocket, raising his eyebrow at the rubber-banded money.

"I guess Walter set you up pretty well. Still, this doesn't mean anything. I'm guessing you've got the data addresses memorized. Lucky for you, I'm still willing to trade. We'll go up to the cabin just like I planned. Let you think for a few hours, let you get a little twitchier. . . ." He glanced at his watch. "Yeah, give it an hour or two and you should be pretty cooperative. You tell me what I need to know, I give you the antidote." He dug into his pocket, pulled out a syringe, and held it up to show her before putting it back. "I used the spare on your boyfriend here, so he can confirm it's the good stuff. Anyway, then I call up my guys, make the trade, and it's happily ever after for everyone. I'll be on a beach next week with eight million in offshore accounts, and you two can go to prom together."

"It's hardly happily ever after for the Albanians' future victims," Tanner said angrily. "You're going to arm them with a weapon no one can control."

Baxter shrugged, faking a yawn. "Me, or someone else. News flash, kid: the world's an unstable place. There's a global marketplace for terror, and you can either get your piece or let it run you over. If it isn't me, someone else will sell it."

"Not if the Army Criminal Investigation Command shuts down the lab," Carina spat. "Did you threaten my mom because she got too close?"

"Oh, that. That was ridiculously easy." Baxter laughed. "I was in it for the long haul. I was willing to wait until they figured out the little problem of how to attach the antidote. The virus without the antidote wasn't worth a fraction of what I'm going to get for it now. But then your mom started nosing around, trying to get the whole project shut down. Well, I couldn't have that, now, could I?"

The knot of grief that Carina had buried deep inside threatened to burst free. She knew that if she allowed rage to overtake her now, she couldn't do what needed to be done. So she pushed it back down. "How did you stop her?" she asked quietly, tasting bile.

He shook his head, as though he couldn't believe it himself. "One phone call. I used a voice mod—told her if she didn't get the hell out of Dodge I was going after you. Said if I ever saw her face again I'd take you out. Hell, I never thought it would be so easy to scare her off. That's the problem with women," he added offhandedly. "Too sentimental. Your mom, Sheila, both of them let their feelings for you get in the way of what matters."

"It's not just women," Tanner said, his voice like steel. "You don't get to decide who matters. We're going to beat you, Baxter. I don't know when and I don't know how, but we're going to walk away from this and you're not."

Baxter laughed. "Yeah, really? 'Cause if I'm not mistaken, I'm the guy with the gun here and you're just the little punk caught with his pants down."

Still chuckling, he moved around to the back of the car and popped the trunk.

"There's someone I'd like you to meet, Carina," he added. "Just in case you're considering using your superhero powers on poor little old mortal me."

A man rose from the trunk, unfolding his limbs and flexing his hands, working the kinks out of his neck and shoulders. He leapt lightly to the ground, a young, fit man dressed in camouflage clothes and boots. Carina recognized the flushed skin, the bright eyes, the manic quality of his expression.

He'd been infected.

"Meet Joe," Baxter said. "Not your average gun for hire. All you need to know is that anything you can do, he can do better. So mind your manners."

CHAPTER NINETEEN

Saturday, 6:20 a.m.
RESET: 02:38:42

"Joe"—Carina was pretty sure that wasn't his real name—rode in the backseat with Carina and Tanner on either side, like a parent separating two quarrelsome toddlers. Baxter drove. In what seemed like moments, they were on the Bay Bridge, heading out of San Francisco into the East Bay under the early-morning sunrise.

It had been eleven hours since she and Tanner had taken the BART train under this very same body of water on their way to Uncle Walter's secret hideaway. Three hours since Tanner had killed a man. A little more than an hour since they'd nearly been blown up by a drone.

It was now only a little over two hours until she started to die.

She wondered what it would feel like. Right now, she

could sense her pulse racing far faster than normal. Her face was sheened with perspiration, and if it hadn't been for the water bottles from the trunk that Baxter had tossed to them earlier, she was sure she would have started to experience dehydration. In addition to processing calories at an astonishing rate, she sensed that her body was burning through water, and she drank two bottles in a row.

She was famished again, but her hunger took a backseat to other sensations, none of them pleasant. Some of the larger muscles in her arms and legs had begun twitching uncontrollably. Not often—just enough to make her notice—but she had a feeling that the pace would only increase. She was starting to have trouble focusing on a single thought at a time. Her senses were in overdrive: the colors in the view out the window—the cerulean sky, the white sails dotting the navy of the water, the red car in the next lane—hurt her eyes. She was assaulted by dozens of odors with each inhalation: not just the cologne, deodorant, sweat, and soap smells of the other passengers, but chemical smells of carpet shampoo and window cleaner and leather conditioner; coffee and stale food that must have been consumed in the car; and a dozen different notes in the air circulating from the outside. In addition to the sound of the engine and the passing traffic, she could hear the breathing of each individual; she even heard her own heartbeat.

It was too much, overwhelming. She thought back to the video of the agitated young man before he started to harm himself. She would know how he felt—soon, unless she was able to get the antidote. But what were the odds of that happening, really? Even if she and Tanner handed over the IP address on the ring and the password generator—even if Baxter had proof that he now had access to all of Walter's data—what motivation did he have to keep her alive? He'd already proved several times over that he was not afraid to take human lives. He'd dispatched Sheila, a woman he'd known for years, without a second thought. Why would he care about killing two more?

Even if, by some sheer stroke of luck, he decided to spare Carina, he had nothing at all invested in Tanner. Tanner was just an ordinary teen, now that he'd received the antidote; he was an innocent. Carina managed to steal a few glances at him as the car sped east. He looked calm, his complexion restored, but he had a look of concern in his eyes when he returned her glance; he showed no fear other than his worry for her. He must have known that he was doomed, but he seemed to accept his fate calmly.

Carina heard a soft tearing sound and looked down at her hands. She had been gripping the seat on either side, and without realizing it had actually managed to rip it open in two places as she thought about Tanner. The foam innards of the seat pushed against the fabric upholstery. Joe glanced over with his eyebrows raised above the mirrored sunglasses he slipped on; when he saw what Carina had done, she thought she detected a faint smirk on his face. No one else seemed to notice.

Carina wondered if Joe had hurt people before, if that was part of his job description. Even if he had, being infected made him many times more deadly. It was what the virus had been developed for, after all. That and defense, but Carina would bet that when the Calaveras Lab people made their pitch, when they described all the ways the armed services could use the virus to increase the efficiency of their troops, the thought on everyone's mind was the on-the-ground conflicts plaguing war-torn nations the world over. How appealing would it be to think of sending troops home alive instead of in body bags? Of lowering the incidences of civilian casualties and friendly-fire events? Of turning the tide on drug wars being waged near the nation's borders?

But there was the other side to consider. A force like this could not be contained. It hadn't even been perfected, and it was already leaking out to the wrong side, all because of a single disgruntled and greedy employee. You could never prevent that kind of sabotage. If the virus was released into the world, it would certainly find its way to all sides of the conflict.

And increasing the skill sets of both sides of a battle had to result in more dead—not fewer.

Tanner was as good as dead. Carina probably was too. In their possession was the key to evil on a scale she could only imagine. Maybe it was time, finally, to give up. To destroy the seeds of ruin, even if it meant destroying themselves.

They were passing the midpoint of the bridge, the span over Treasure Island. It was another couple of miles before they finished crossing the bay and then another hour to get to the wilderness where the cabin was located.

Carina knew she was no match for Joe once they got out of the car. They were both infected, but he was still in the early stages, with more precise control of his body. Plus, he had several inches and fifty pounds on her.

But if she acted now . . .

All it would take was one deliberate move. If she threw herself at the front seat, grabbed the wheel, she could send them through the guardrail. They were going fast enough for the momentum to easily carry them through the barrier and into the water. And even if any of them somehow made it out alive, the password generator would be destroyed. The data would be lost.

Carina closed her eyes, breathing in and out as calmly as she could. She willed her heartbeat to stabilize; imagined her muscles relaxing, her breathing slowing, just as she did before track meets.

And a thought came to her.

An idea so audacious, so risky, that she had no idea where it had come from. Her eyes flew open and her lips parted. It was crazy, it probably wouldn't work, but it gave them a chance.

A chance to save Tanner was all she needed.

"Oh, all right," she said quietly, in a defeated tone. "I have what you want. But it's back in Martindale."

CHAPTER TWENTY

Saturday, 7:38 a.m.
01:21:47

Tanner carefully kept his eyes forward. Carina knew he had to be wondering what she was up to, but he didn't dare give her away.

"It's at my school," Carina improvised. It was Saturday; the janitors would have finished their weekend duties yesterday. If she was lucky, the school would be abandoned; it was unlikely any teachers would be catching up on their work this early in the morning.

Requirements for a showdown with an armed sociopath and an infected mercenary? Large, open area—check. Minimization of potential for civilian casualties—check. Possibilities for those who were neither mercenaries nor infected—like Tanner, for instance—to get the hell out of the way—again, she hoped, check.

It wasn't much of a plan, except for one thing. In the cabin, they were certainly doomed. Baxter had all the advantages: he knew the layout, surroundings, and terrain. He probably had additional weapons there, as well as a plan for disposing of their bodies.

At the school, she could make it a fairer fight. She knew every inch of the campus, since her training had taken her everywhere from the basement stairwell when they'd trained indoors on rainy days to the farthest corner of the freshman practice field.

"What exactly are you offering to give me?"

Carina slipped off her ring. She stared at it for a moment, allowing herself to remember her mother's embrace last night, the way her eyes had softened when she'd looked at Carina. She pressed the green stone to her lips, a final kiss.

Then she handed it over the seat. Baxter took it, never taking his eyes off the road.

"That's my mom's ring. Inscribed inside, underneath the stone, is an IP address. My uncle used an overseas VPN to back up all of his work. It's all there, don't worry, we checked."

"How do you get in?" Baxter didn't bother to conceal the excitement in his voice.

"You need a password," Carina said. "It's generated by a device I hid at the school. It creates a new password every few seconds, automatically syncing with the server. It's the only one—if there's another way to get in, it died with Walter."

"Two-factor authentication," Baxter said, whistling through his teeth. "Nice. What did you do, hide it in your locker?"

"Are you kidding?" Carina said, thinking fast. "They can do random searches these days, did you know that? Civil liberties don't extend to kids, apparently."

"Poor you," Baxter said drily. "So where'd you stash it?"

"On the roof." Carina could feel herself flush. She didn't dare look at Tanner. "There's a heating and air-conditioning unit up there, and I hid it inside."

"Exposed to the elements?" Baxter said sharply. "Are you insane?"

"No, of course not. It's well protected—you're just going to have to trust me on that."

"That's a lot of trust you're asking for, little girl."

"Well," Carina said with a confidence she didn't feel, "if it turns out I'm wrong, what do you lose? You can let me die as easily in the high school parking lot as a cabin in the woods, right?"

Baxter nodded slowly. "I guess that would work, even if it would be a little messy. By the time you started creating a public disturbance and the police answered the call, your communication faculties would be gone. Your heart rate would be up over one fifty, and if you didn't stroke out, organ shutdown would follow. Give the ER docs the shock of a lifetime. And I'd love to see how fast the lab would cover that up. Of course, you know I wouldn't be able to let Tanner go. It'd be back to plan A for him: the bottom of the lake."

"That's not going to happen," Carina said. "I give you the password generator, you let us go. Right?"

"Right."

They were each lying to the other, Carina thought as the

early-morning traffic moved slowly along Highway 24. At this rate, it would be an hour's drive back to the high school. The beautiful green foothills were dotted with wildflowers, and a few fluffy clouds scuttled across the sky. It was a perfect spring day, the kind that had always made her grateful to live in the area.

And to think she had been considering going to Cal State Long Beach. The ocean had a certain appeal, of course, but she would miss the rugged beauty of the coastal range, the mountains she'd grown up with. On the other side was Berkeley ... and, for that matter, Alta Vista Community College. If she'd applied to Alta Vista instead of Long Beach, she would have been twenty minutes from Tanner, close enough to see him as often as she wanted.

How had it taken this long for her to realize that what mattered most was being near Tanner? She could have thrived at Alta Vista. A few kids from her school would be attending; she would have been able to find a roommate easily.

It was a perfect fantasy, so Carina was almost surprised by the tears pricking her eyes. Well, she would make one part of it true, at least. Tanner would attend Berkeley next fall. He was healthy, he had received the antidote. In time— maybe not next year or the year after that, but eventually— he would put this behind him.

All he had to do was remember the door that led from the roof into the building. On the night they'd made love, she and Tanner had discovered that the door was propped open. A scattering of cigarette butts revealed why: someone made a regular habit of going up on the roof to smoke. The door locked from the inside, which was probably why the smoker used an old paint can to keep it open, to make sure he could get back in.

As long as Tanner could get through the door and close it, he'd be safe. Sure, it was possible—even likely—that Joe could force his way through the door somehow, but Carina would be willing to bet that Baxter would prefer to use his rent-a-soldier to keep tabs on her. The loss of Tanner would anger him, no doubt, but not enough to distract him from his mission.

And not nearly as much as discovering that Carina had led him on a wild-goose chase. She squeezed her eyes shut. Well, once Tanner was safe, there was a handy way to make sure that she didn't suffer an agonizing death. An easy out, right over the edge of the roof. She wouldn't survive a four-story drop, and her death would be instantaneous. Painless.

Traffic cleared when they passed through Walnut Creek and continued southeast toward the Central Valley. Carina watched the familiar sights going by, knowing she probably wouldn't ever see any of them again. The mall where she'd shopped with her friends. A rival high school, where she'd attended half a dozen track meets. A park Uncle Walter had taken her to when she was little.

And then they were inside the Martindale town limits. It looked so ordinary, so peaceful. Yesterday, when she woke up, it had seemed all wrong that her town should look so serene on the day she would be burying her uncle. She'd resented the well-dressed crowd of mourners; every smile, every pleasant word had been an affront to her sadness. She'd resented Sheila—and how wrong she had been about that. Walter too. They'd misjudged the awkward, reserved woman who ended up losing her life because she tried to help.

All three of them were gone: her mother, her uncle, and now Sheila. Everyone who cared about Carina ended up dead.

No more.

Carina bit down on her lip hard enough to taste blood. Good. The blood was a reminder that she would embrace violence, if violence was what it took to end this. A little bloodshed now to avoid the loss of countless innocent people later on the soil of Albania and other conflict-torn lands, places where the strong prevailed and the weak perished. Carina would not allow the virus to add to the tally of the dead. A small victory, perhaps, but one she was willing to fight for.

The high school loomed ahead. One of the oldest buildings in town, the four-story stone edifice had survived the tremors of the 1906 earthquake centered thirty miles away. New buildings had been added to the campus over the years; the auditorium hailed from the sixties, the pool and gymnasium from the eighties. But Carina loved the old main building best.

She would have graduated from Martindale High this June, and Baxter had been right—she would have attended the prom with Tanner. Carina had been looking at dresses in department store windows since early spring. If all of this hadn't happened, she might have gone shopping with Emma and Nikki, Walter's credit card in her purse, and picked out a dress in turquoise blue, because Tanner said he liked that shade best on her. She would have worn her hair up, and her mother's ring.

Carina inhaled sharply. She couldn't lose focus now.

"Pull around the side," she directed Baxter. There were only a few other cars in the parking lot, none of them familiar. Out on the field, a pair of middle-aged women in velour sweat suits walked laps around the track.

Baxter parked near the edge of the lot. Carina wondered whether an expensive sedan with tinted windows would raise eyebrows. Surely if anyone saw them get out—a young, handsome man in a suit and another in camouflage, accompanied by two high school students—they would take notice. But this side of the high school backed up to the foothills, and there were no houses, no walking paths, no traffic to see them.

Baxter held Carina's door open. She got out stiffly. The tremors were getting closer together, tiny seizures electrifying her nerves up and down her limbs. There was an unpleasant metallic taste in her mouth that swallowing could not get rid of. Her skin prickled along the tops of her arms, on the back of her neck and scalp, and she had to resist the urge to scratch. She remembered the test subject's frantic attack on himself, his fingers bloodied, and shuddered with revulsion and fear.

Joe maneuvered his considerable bulk out of the car and

waited for Tanner to follow. Tanner got out and came directly to Carina, putting his arms around her.

"Hey," Baxter said, but Tanner ignored him, holding Carina close.

"Are you really okay?" Carina whispered, inhaling his scent and pressing her face into his neck.

"Yeah, I feel almost normal. Still a little amped up, like I've had five cups of coffee. Nothing worse than that. I bet I'm in for a hell of a crash, though."

Carina winced at his word choice. She wished she could communicate her plan to him—but she couldn't say anything in front of Joe or Baxter.

"What about you?" he murmured.

"Fine," Carina lied as firmly as she could, gritting her teeth and tensing her muscles so that Tanner wouldn't feel the trembling and tics, and forced a smile.

Baxter gave Tanner a disgusted shove. "Enough of that. Joe, help our friend here pay attention."

Joe put his hands under Tanner's arms, picking him off the ground as though he weighed no more than a bouquet of flowers. Tanner's feet dangled but he didn't react, didn't say anything, and after a second Joe let him drop. Just proving a point.

"You first," Baxter told Carina, pointing to the fire escape. "Then Joe. I'll climb up behind Tanner. You won't give me any trouble, will you, buddy?"

Tanner didn't answer, even though Baxter had his gun out. Not taking any chances, even though Tanner was no longer infected.

Smart move, Carina thought; she wouldn't count Tanner out.

She led the way to the fire escape, her heart racing in a ragged rhythm. Sawhorses and caution signs had been set up around the bottom. Joe picked them up like toothpicks and tossed them out of the way.

"Up you go," Baxter said.

Carina put her hand on the lowest rung, the metal cold and rough in her grip, and turned to look at the others. If she were alone, she'd have risked making a dash for it—her supercharged body could have easily tackled the climb in record time. She'd bet she would have had a fifty-fifty chance that Baxter could take aim and hit her before she got to the roof, and if she'd managed to get a head start she could probably have beaten Joe too. He was bigger than her, but that might actually have worked against him, all other things being equal, once they were on the flat ground of the roof. Carina would have sprinted like hell, and she just might have been able to outrun him.

But with Tanner on the ground, she couldn't even consider bolting. Not when Baxter might shoot him out of spite as quickly as he would for cause.

Carina climbed slowly. She felt the structure shudder when Joe pulled himself onto the bottom rungs; moments later it did so two more times when Tanner and Baxter started to climb.

Joe stayed within inches of her, silent except for the clanging of his hands and feet on the metal rungs. Behind him, she could hear Tanner's and Baxter's breathing as they ascended with less precision and efficiency. With her heightened senses, Carina was conscious of the stark differences between those like her and ordinary, uninfected humans. To her acute hearing, the breathing of even fit men like Tanner and Baxter sounded labored.

She reached the top and pulled herself up and over the low wall at the edge. Her foot slipped when it hit the roof, trembling so badly that it had buckled on impact. Her body was beginning to deteriorate. Carina swallowed down her panic; if she couldn't depend on her reactions, how could she carry out her plan?

She took a couple more steps and waited. Joe, cresting the edge, looked unruffled. His footsteps were sure, his motions perfectly economical. He'd probably received his injection right before climbing into the trunk of the car; he couldn't have been infected for more than a few hours.

Joe stared directly into her eyes. His expression betrayed no emotion at all.

"You proud of yourself, picking on kids?" Carina asked. She knew she ought to keep her mouth shut, that nothing she said could help in this situation. "How much did he have to pay you, anyway? And why are you so sure he's going to take care of you afterward? That he's going to give you the antidote?"

The man just stared at her, hands hanging loosely at his sides. Over the side of the building, she heard Tanner and Baxter approaching the top of the ladder, their labored breathing punctuated by grunts of effort. They'd made the climb quickly—much more quickly than she and Tanner had a few nights ago, when it felt like they had all the time in the world—and they would be winded when they reached the top.

Good.

"You know what happens, don't you, if you don't get the antidote?" she demanded. Joe lifted one thick eyebrow and regarded her curiously.

"*Qepe gojën.*"

CHAPTER TWENTY-ONE

Saturday, 8:38 a.m.
0:21:11

Carina gasped. The man was foreign. Albanian, she'd bet. He hadn't been following Baxter's commands at all, but rather directions he'd been given before coming on this mission. *Don't let the girl escape,* no doubt—and probably *Kill anyone who interferes.* Simple, really, when it came down to it.

What had happened since she and Tanner had left one Albanian in a pool of his own blood and the other choking in a drainage pipe? Clearly, allegiances had shifted. A deal had been brokered. Baxter was full of surprises: somehow, in the space of hours, he'd convinced the Albanians not to kill Carina and gotten an extension on the exchange timetable— and they'd thrown in a strongman to sweeten the deal.

Tanner came over the edge, panting. He looked exhausted, deep purple pockets under his eyes, his skin pale and sheened with perspiration. No wonder: he hadn't slept, and he'd been putting his body through exertions that—chemically enhanced or otherwise—would take time to recover from.

But he smiled. The minute he saw that she was unhurt, he smiled as though nothing was wrong. He reached for her hand and squeezed, and when Joe shoved him hard enough that he stumbled against the parapet, the smile still never left his face.

Baxter was another story, scowling with annoyance when he finally came up on the roof. Getting shown up by a girl, perhaps, or having to keep Tanner alive long enough to get what he wanted from Carina, was wearing on his nerves. Whatever the case, he didn't look happy.

"Okay," he said, breathing hard. "So where is it?"

This was it—the moment of truth. If Carina pulled this off, Tanner was safe. If not ... well, there simply couldn't be an *if not.*

"This way," Carina said. "Around here."

She led them toward the cluster of HVAC equipment near the center of the roof, all enclosed in a boxy, painted metal structure. It was only a few yards away from the door leading into the stairwell at the top of the building, the one that promised escape for Tanner. Thankfully, lodged in the space between door and frame was the same crusty paint can that had been there the other day.

Carina moved slowly, making sure the rest of the little group was keeping pace. Joe was shadowing her so tightly that she wouldn't be able to get away with anything. Once she started fumbling around among the curved pipes that made up the HVAC exhaust system, she'd have little time; it would soon become obvious that she'd been lying. *I can't imagine what happened to it,* she'd say. *It was here two days ago, I swear.* Sure. That might get her a few extra minutes. But the end was inevitable: the minute Tanner made it inside the building and locked the door, she was finished. She wouldn't even risk a last look in his direction; she'd race straight to the edge.

Over. Down. Dead.

And the virus would finally be finished. If Tanner made it out, he would call the major, the investigation would be launched, the lab shut down; and if the Albanian connection somehow escaped notice, it hardly mattered. Baxter was right about one thing: evil would continue to exist in the world no matter what happened today.

They arrived at the HVAC unit. Carina laid a hand on the side, feeling the warmth of the sun on the metal. She looked at Tanner, who was lagging back just as he needed to. Good—so he understood. She stared pointedly into his eyes and then at the propped-open door, then down at the metal assemblage, making her meaning clear: when she started searching for the item that wasn't there, Baxter's attention would be diverted, and Tanner could run for the door. He only had to cross a distance of about five yards, and the second he was behind the door—reinforced metal, with a heavy dead bolt—he was safe. Baxter wouldn't be able to shoot through it, at least not in time to catch him, even if he was a normal teenager now. Baxter wouldn't send

Joe after him until she was disposed of, so all Tanner had to do was race down four flights of stairs and out any exit. That would set off the building alarms, so with any luck at all, the police would arrive in time to find Baxter and Joe before they could make it off the roof.

And Carina's body, broken and bleeding on the ground below. But there was no point to thinking about that.

She knelt. "Well, let's see, I put it behind one of these vertical pipes," Carina said, making a show of sliding her hands behind the filthy metal pieces. *Now,* she willed Tanner. *Go.* He edged carefully back from Baxter—good.

But he wasn't moving toward the door.

Carina's heart seized with horror as she saw that he was moving toward a stack of construction debris near the edge of the HVAC enclosure. What was he doing? There wasn't any way to get down on that side, no ladder, no door.

"Maybe it was over here," Carina mumbled, running her hands into each recessed space between the bars, trying to keep the panic out of her voice. She had only seconds before they realized there was nothing here, that she had led them on a wild-goose chase.

Tanner took off, sprinting the last few feet to the pile of lumber and rusting metal. Joe pivoted instantly at the sound of footsteps, responding with virus-heightened instinct. As Tanner crouched down in front of it he yelled, "*Run,* Car!" at the top of his lungs. Baxter yowled with frustration as he tried to find a shot, but Tanner had taken cover just in time.

Carina stood, tearing her eyes away from Tanner. For one second her gaze locked on Joe's. His eyes were clear, intent, and bright; his neutral expression had given way to the slightest smirk.

Try me, it said.

Carina ran.

She focused all the skittering energy that pulsed through her veins and synapses and nerves. She imagined them as strands dancing and jerking with life, and in her mind she drew them all together to make one strong cord, knitting the virus's powerful side effects into a single rope of pure strength and determination. By pushing herself as hard as she could, she managed to stop the spasming and twitching in her muscles. She knew she couldn't sustain her pace for long, but she only needed a few seconds more.

Her takeoff was flawless, and each step landed exactly where it needed to. Her arms pumped at her side. Her hair streamed in the wind, the unfamiliar sensation of her shorn strands fluttering against her neck. She had a lead of a few yards on Joe, and she suspected he could close that gap, given his greater musculature and the fact that he was earlier in the infection's course. But she had a fighting chance.

Because when she reached the edge of the roof, she was going to jump. The space between the main building and the auditorium was about five yards, a little less than the women's long-jump record. It didn't really matter, of course, whether Carina landed the jump or not; she was still as good as dead, but getting to the other roof might buy her a few more minutes that she could use to find out what happened to Tanner. Because now it was him against Baxter, and even though Baxter had a gun, she figured it was an even fight. Tanner might not be armed, and he was exhausted, but he had a few things Baxter didn't: heart, and courage—and love.

The edge. The parapet rose up three feet, its surface slick with tar and bird droppings. The top was curved and would not provide good purchase, but she needed to anchor on it nonetheless for her leap. She could hear her coach's voice in her mind: *The greater the speed at takeoff, the longer the trajectory of the center of mass....*

She hurtled forward, her feet striking the ground in perfectly spaced strides. She pushed off and hit the top of the wall with her right foot, imagining every winning approach and every record-breaking jump she'd ever landed.

And then she was airborne.

As she passed over the space below, time stretched and somehow made room for a stream of memories: arriving at the doors of the high school on the first day of freshman year, her new backpack still stiff and stuffed with supplies and books, her hair soft and shiny from an hour with the blow dryer, wishing she could both disappear and be noticed. Eating lunch with Nikki and Emma under the sycamore tree during their sophomore year. Surrounded by kids the day she came back to school after Madelyn's funeral in her junior year, the center of a hug that seemed to encompass a hundred students. Hanging out on the benches near the entrance after school the Monday after she met Tanner last fall, telling Nikki and Emma about the amazing boy from the climbing gym.

The shock of the impact traveled through her, from the

bones in her feet up through her entire body to her fingers. It wasn't a perfect landing, but she knew within a microsecond that she was unhurt, and she dove into a roll and came up facing backward, already frantically searching for Tanner.

A thud next to her alerted her that Joe had made the jump as well. But his pained grunt indicated that it had cost him. Without training in the mechanics of the long jump, he had undoubtedly made any of a dozen mistakes that could lead to injury. Carina prayed he'd broken his ankle, but before she could find out she had to see Tanner.

There he was, arm stretched back, a stance he'd perfected training for the javelin throw. Baxter had his gun in hand and was turning back toward Tanner, preparing to shoot. Carina's gaze sharpened and intensified, the splintering effects of the aging virus bringing the scene into surreal focus. She saw Baxter's finger tighten on the trigger just as she saw Tanner release the iron rebar that he'd been holding.

She couldn't trace the path of the bullet, though the sound Tanner made when it struck, forcing him backward, was proof it had hit home. She could, however, follow the arc of the rebar. It soared straight through the air toward Baxter and impaled him through the right shoulder. She heard his gun clatter to the roof a millisecond before he started screaming.

Tanner was on his feet. His left arm bloomed red near the elbow and hung at an odd angle, but the bullet didn't stop him from lurching forward and kneeling in front of Baxter.

Next to Carina, Joe made sounds like an angry bull as he crawled toward her, dragging one leg. He would reach her in seconds, and Carina knew she had to run, but she couldn't tear her eyes away from Tanner. He crouched over the writhing, screaming form of Baxter, and then he stood, his good arm winding up for a throw.

"Catch!" he screamed.

She didn't.

The little vial glanced off her fingers and fell to the roof, but it didn't break. Tanner's aim had been perfect, but Carina's fingers were shaking badly now, unsteadied by the virus or maybe just the combination of fear and adrenaline. Carina seized the vial and tore off the plastic safety cap. The exposed needle glinted in the sun, and she jammed it into her thigh, the auto-delivery mechanism snapping on impact, delivering the dose of antidote straight into her muscle as Joe pulled himself to his feet and staggered toward her.

The needle stung, but Carina ignored the pain as she forced herself to stand, and then began to run.

Tanner would live. His arm looked bad, but there was no way Baxter would chase him now. He was writhing and screaming, trying to pull the rebar from his shoulder. The sound of a gunshot confirmed that Tanner had retrieved Baxter's gun and was trying to stop Joe, but thudding footsteps behind Carina indicated he had missed.

She took a chance and looked around. The giant man had managed to get to his feet and was pursuing her, a slight limp the only evidence of damage to his leg. She wondered if the antidote had already slowed her, if the virus was abandoning her system and leaving her worn, tired, spent. *Slow.* As Joe closed the gap between them, his limp seemed to diminish before her eyes. The virus at work, or merely the man's will? Either way, he would catch up to her in seconds.

Carina had never guessed that she could make the jump between buildings. If she had, she might have conceived the ending of her plan much earlier. She'd only envisioned one possible ending for herself then, and it involved the intersection of her body and the concrete sidewalk.

But now she had another option.

Up ahead, past the rooftops, was the field in which Carina had spent countless afternoons training. There was the outer curve of the track, the visitor stands, the snack shack that was shuttered and locked now but during football season bustled with activity.

One last time Carina looked out over the visitor stands, the hills behind dotted with beautiful old oak trees. She fixed the image in her mind, calculated the distance to the edge of the roof, and took the last few steps with all the power she could muster.

One final time, the waning virus slowed the passage of seconds, and she pictured her last track practice before Walter had died. She'd been working on her high-jump landing. It was her weakest event, and she'd struggled over the course of the season. Again and again, she threw her body over the bar, landing on the thick blue mat. She'd made that jump so many times, and while she waited her turn behind her teammates, Carina had time to notice how the mat nearly touched the water cart on the left, how its seams were splitting in one spot near the tag along the bottom.

How it lined up perfectly with the right edge of the visitor stands.

And as Carina's foot touched off the edge of the roof, she was staring at that same spot in the stands, praying hard that no one had moved the mat.

It felt as though she'd been falling forever. The breath was knocked out of her on impact, and sharp agony racked her rib cage. The worst pain was in her right leg. Lifting her head to check on it, she saw stars, and lay back down.

She'd also seen blue—the bright blue of the high-jump mat. She was sprawled across it and, broken bones or not, she was alive.

But the mat wasn't all she'd seen.

Lying next to it, on the track, were the remains of one very dead Albanian.

EPILOGUE

Carina adjusted the hem of her scarlet graduation gown. It kept catching on her cast, the slippery fabric snagging on the sharp edges. It was taking forever for the three hundred seniors to walk, one by one, up onto the stage to receive their diplomas. By the time they finally reached the Ms, Carina was perspiring under the hot June sun. The boy who'd been sitting two seats down from her, Edward Mankowicz, made fake gang signs at the assembled crowd as he took his time crossing the stage. There were a few disapproving murmurs, and the vice principal's smile slipped.

But nothing could dampen Carina's mood today. She was officially graduating from Martindale High, Class of 2013, despite having missed nearly two weeks of her final semester: the week after Walter died and a week recovering from a broken fibula, two broken ribs, a fractured ankle, and a mild concussion after her fall from the roof of the high school auditorium.

"Nastyshakes," Carina whispered, pretending to adjust the strap of her shoe so no one would hear, not that it was likely anyway over the din of the excited seniors. "Cover FX. And Tanner."

Nastyshakes was Mrs. Sloan's secret recipe, a combination of wheatgrass, Greek yogurt, kale, and a variety of other ingredients that looked disgusting on the kitchen counter. Somehow, though, when she poured them out of the blender, the combination tasted delicious and did everything she promised, calming Carina's nerves and giving her energy. Carina had been too nervous this morning to eat anything else, and Mrs. Sloan—thrilled to finally have a girl living in the house—had served her in a crystal glass to celebrate the occasion.

The Cover FX makeup was also a gift from Mrs. Sloan. Just a few strokes of the thick cream covered the evidence of the injuries Carina suffered in the fall. The jagged scar on her cheek was still healing, but the doctors assured her it would eventually be far less noticeable. Meanwhile, the Cover FX guaranteed that her graduation and prom pictures wouldn't be marred by any reminders of the infection and its fallout.

And then there was Tanner, who was out there somewhere in the audience with his family. Last night at Tanner's own graduation from Borden School, it had been Carina who sat in the stands. Tanner's brothers had grumbled about having to sit through two incredibly boring ceremonies, but Mr. Sloan had silenced them by saying that if they didn't behave they wouldn't be allowed to participate in the family paintball battle, which he had announced was a new graduation weekend tradition for all graduating Sloans and honorary Sloans, including Carina.

Not to be outdone, Mrs. Sloan was hosting the first traditional Sloan family graduation tea this afternoon for the moms from Tanner's school. Carina had helped her polish the silver and set the table. As Mrs. Sloan put the finishing touches on the floral centerpiece, she abruptly dragged Carina into a hug. "I wish your mom could be here," she whispered fiercely, "but I want you to know you're like a daughter to me. I hope you'll consider this your home forever." She'd brushed at her eyes impatiently, then added, "No matter what happens with you and Tanner."

Carina had mumbled her thanks. When Mrs. Sloan excused herself to go find a tissue, Carina tucked a loose snapdragon into the arrangement and wondered how she'd lucked into this family.

It was time for her to put her grief on the back shelf for now. Carina knew it would never go away completely. Especially in the case of her mother: there had been nothing in the paper, no announcement of a body found in an abandoned house in South San Francisco. Maybe the Albanians had disposed of it. Or maybe ... It was so tempting to wonder if Madelyn had somehow survived. The bullet might have missed her heart, might have somehow missed all of her vital organs. Maybe even now she was on the run again, still trying to escape the deadly shadow of Project Venice, even after it had been officially shut down, with the lab under very public review by the Army Criminal Investigation Command.

But Carina needed to move on. Mr. Sloan had spent almost two hours with her the other day, going over her course selections at Alta Vista Community College and reviewing the requirements for transferring to UC Berkeley in a couple of years. The Sloans had also cosigned the lease on an apartment she would be sharing with two other girls, and accompanied Carina to appointments with the attorney handling her uncle's estate.

As for Tanner ... Privacy was in short supply in a family with four boys, especially when the three youngest hooted and pretended to throw up whenever Tanner held Carina's hand or snuck a kiss. Only once since she had been released from the hospital had they snuck away for an entire evening by themselves. There would be plenty of opportunities later, when they started school.

Meanwhile, they had become masters of the stolen moment.

This morning, Tanner had knocked on her door after Mr. Sloan gave his customary ten-minute warning: standing at the bottom of the stairs and yelling that if anyone wasn't ready, he was leaving them behind. Carina opened the bedroom door, zipping up the dress she was wearing under her gown.

Tanner handed her a small white box. Inside was her mother's ring.

"Oh, Tanner . . . I never thought I'd see this again."

"The cops sent it over last week, after they got done processing the crime scene. Mom thought . . . well, we took it to the jewelers. Here, open it."

Carina slid her finger under the special prong, and the stone lifted.

The rows of numerals were gone, smoothed away in the gold. In their place were initials in flowing script: CM & TS.

This time, she had no hesitation at all. "I love you," she said, before he could say anything. "I always will. I have since the day we met."

《◆》

As Edward Mankowicz finally strutted off the stage and Jill Maurice started across, wobbling on her high heels, Carina twisted the ring on her finger. It was time. She took a deep breath and stood, picking up her crutches. The trip down the aisle and up the steps to the stage was a slow one, and she felt her face flush as she focused on not tripping. She concentrated on putting one foot in front of the other as she walked across the wooden platform, barely aware of shaking the vice principal's hand or tucking the diploma under her arm. Only when she was back in her seat did she dare look out into the crowd, searching for Tanner and his family.

A flash of red caught her eye. There—in the shadow of the stands—a female figure hesitated for a moment, her thick red hair partially obscuring her face.

It looked a lot like her mother—same lean, angular build; same pronounced cheekbones under the oversize sunglasses—but from this distance, the resemblance could easily have been Carina's imagination. She forced herself to breathe, and squeezed her hands together in her lap as the vice principal read the next name from her list and the audience clapped politely.

How many times had Carina wished for a miracle? Even though she'd seen her shot, Carina had kept a tiny, secret hope alive that her mother had survived. Everyone involved in Project Venice was either in jail or dead. Major Wynnside was overseeing a massive investigation of every project undertaken by the lab in the last three years. The token generator had survived being stashed in Tanner's sock, and now Walter's research was in good hands, protected with every resource at the government's disposal.

In time, Project Venice would fade from Carina's thoughts, but she would probably spend the rest of her life wondering, every time she saw a woman who resembled her mother, if it really was her. She doubted she'd ever stop missing her.

Being an orphan was something that took a long time to get used to. There were days she was furious with her mother and Walter, days when she wished they could have been accountants or teachers or janitors—any job at all, as long as it was safe.

But the Monroe legacy did not prepare a person for safe choices. There was something in the bloodline that was attracted to risk and danger and the unknown. Project Venice had been irresistible to her mother and uncle, and now Carina was following in their footsteps. She was taking classes to fulfill her general education requirements this fall at Alta Vista, and with a little luck, in two years she would enter UC Berkeley as a mathematics major focusing on cryptography, studying under many of the most prominent data security experts in the country. Once she graduated, she would find herself in some agency dedicated to keeping the country safe, and that kind of commitment didn't come without real risk.

The red-haired figure disappeared from view. But there, in the middle of the bleachers, a bright flash of sun caught Carina's eye, and a small hand waved frantically at her. It was Caleb, Tanner's youngest brother, wearing the mirrored sunglasses Carina had bought him on a family outing to an amusement park.

And there, wedged between his little brothers, was Tanner. He was too far away for her to see his expression. But she didn't need special powers to know that his smile was the one he reserved for her alone, that his eyes held the love she had come to depend on.

For a day and a half, Carina and Tanner had been among the most powerful humans the world had ever known, capable of astonishing feats of strength and speed. The antidote had made them ordinary again in nearly every way.

Except for one. The bond between them had been strengthened by their ordeal, and nothing would change that. Long after anyone remembered that Tanner and Carina had once been superhuman, their love would live on.

ABOUT THE AUTHOR

Sophie Littlefield grew up in rural Missouri, the middle child of a professor and an artist. She has been writing stories since childhood. After taking a hiatus to raise her two children, she sold her first book in 2008 and has since written more than a dozen novels in several genres. Sophie makes her home in Northern California.